VERSUS

LOVE IN MANHATTAN SERIES

DEBORAH BLADON

FIRST ORIGINAL EDITION, JULY 2019

ISBN: 9781072078685:
eBook ISBN: 9781926440569

Book & cover design by Wolf & Eagle Media

deborahbladon.com

CHAPTER ONE

DYLAN

THE WORLD within Manhattan is its own beast. You learn that when you live here. When you claw your way around this city looking for something elusive.

For some, that's a job that will keep a roof over their heads.

For others, it's a relationship that will stand the test of time and weather the winds of change.

I have the first and no interest in the second.

My needle in the haystack is a particular type of woman.

I don't bother with blondes.

My cock has zero interest in redheads.

For me, it's all about the type of woman I see in front of me now.

Light brown hair, blue eyes, and a petite body that can move to the beat of the music.

Experience has taught me that if a woman can dance, she can fuck.

The woman I'm watching now is graceful, beautiful, and within the hour will be in my bed.

I slide off the bar stool and approach her.

"I'm Dylan."

She taps her ear. "What was that?"

I lean in closer. "I'm Dylan, and you are?"

"Dancing." She breathes on a small laugh.

"You've been watching me." I stand in place while the patrons of this club dance around me, brushing against my expensive, imported suit.

She spins before she slows. "I could say the same for you."

I look down at her face.

Jesus, she's striking. Her eyes are a shade of blue, that particular shade of blue that always takes my breath away.

"We're leaving together tonight."

That cocks one of her perfectly arched brows. "You're assuming that I'm not here with someone."

"You're here alone." I spin when she does to catch her gaze again.

The skirt of her knee-length black dress picks up with the motion revealing a brief flash of her thighs. "Maybe I like being alone."

"Not tonight." I reach for her hand.

She slows before she slides her palm against mine. "Dance with me, Dylan."

I breathe out on a heavy sigh. I haven't heard those four words in years. I haven't danced in as long.

I tug her close to me, sliding my free hand down her back. "What's your name?"

"Does it matter?" She looks up at me.

It never does.

I dance her closer to an alcove, a spot where the crowd is thin and the music quieter.

Her body follows mine instinctively, our shared movements drawing the admiring glances of others.

She's letting me lead now, but the sureness of her steps promises aggression in bed.

"We're wasting time."

Her lips curve up into a smile. "Foreplay comes in many forms."

"Is that what this is?" I laugh. "I want to fuck you."

She presses her body against me. "You will."

My cock swells with those words. "Now."

"Patience, Dylan." Her lips brush my jawline. "I promise this will be a night you'll never forget."

I move to kiss her, but she pulls back, a burst of laughter escaping her.

She's a tease.

I shouldn't find that as alluring as I do. I've walked away from teases before without a glance back, but this woman is intoxicating.

Everything from the sweet scent of her skin to the sound of her voice has me captivated.

I splay my hand over the soft curve at the top of her ass, bringing her even closer. I want her to feel me. I want her to know that I'm hard as stone for her. "Come home with me."

"Home?" She pouts her lips. "I pegged you for the hotel room type."

I study her face. I see something in it that I always look for when I'm ready to take a woman to bed.

It's a flash of familiarity. It may be the curve of a chin or the shape of an eyebrow. This woman has it all.

She's beautiful.

"Hotel rooms are impersonal." I dish out my standard line. "Everything I need is at my apartment."

"You're not going to kidnap me and demand a ransom, are you?" The corner of her mouth twitches in an almost grin.

My cock pulses with each of her subtle movements. We're still dancing. Our rhythm has slowed, but her hips are still in motion, brushing the front of her dress against me.

"Who would I call for the ransom?" I bring her left hand to my mouth, sliding my lips over her bare ring finger. "You're not married, are you?"

Her eyes widen. "I'm not married."

I'm grateful. The need to be inside of her is consuming me.

I have the will to walk away if there's a man waiting somewhere for her, but she's telling the truth.

The years I've spent inside courtrooms have trained me to read people. Sharing my bed with countless women in the past has afforded me the benefit of recognizing guilt in the eyes of someone who has a vested interested in another man.

I've sent women home that have been out prowling the bars of New York City looking for a quick thrill while their husbands are tucking their children into bed.

Revenge sex isn't an interest of mine. I won't be the man that gets you over the inferior son-of-a-bitch that fucked his way into someone else.

If a man cheats on his woman, I want no part of her plan to get even.

I like my sex raw, satisfying, and drama free. I need it to be safe in every possible way.

A good fuck is complicated if hearts are involved.

A barrier of bitterness and regret surrounds mine.

I see no reason to change.

The beauty in my arms stills as the music winds down.

"Promise that you won't try and keep me," she whispers as she looks up at me.

That's a promise I'll gladly keep. "You have my word. One night is all I want."

CHAPTER TWO

DYLAN

"MAYBE I SHOULD BE the one kidnapping you for a ransom," she says from behind me.

I chuckle at that. I watched the way her eyes widened when she caught a glimpse of the bank of windows that greets everyone who enters my apartment.

It was a selling point at the time I bought the place.

I had money to burn and no one but myself to impress.

Three bedrooms, two bathrooms, and a doorman seemed excessive, but investing in real estate is rarely a fool's pursuit.

I've increased my equity since I took possession. The doorman's face has become one of the few constants in my life, and the views of my corner of Manhattan haven't changed enough for me to notice.

I live on Fifth Avenue.

My office is a block over on Madison.

I reap the benefits of other people's misery.

Guilt doesn't factor into that.

If you wake one morning to realize that you don't want to be legally bound to the person next to you in bed, I'm the man you call.

"I assure you no one would pay a ransom for me." I toss my keys on the antique wooden table that houses my home bar.

That consists of a half dozen glass tumblers, an ice bucket that is filled nightly by my assistant, and a bottle of Macallan 15.

Next to that is a manila envelope.

It holds the details of whatever hell awaits me tomorrow. Every night but Friday and Saturday, my assistant prepares his notes for the appointments and cases I'll be dealing with the next day. Divorce as a business is lucrative. Tomorrow will be profitable judging by the thickness of tonight's envelope.

"Don't be so quick to say that." Her gaze trails around the room before it lands on my face. "You must be important to someone."

Watching as she gives me a full once-over, I shove a hand through my black hair.

In the car on the way here she avoided looking at me. Her attention was stolen by the Uber driver who was as infatuated with her as I am.

His small talk about the construction that plagues the city in the spring and summer was annoying and trite, but she found it inviting and intriguing.

At least, that's how it seemed to me as I sat and studied her profile, wondering how anyone can be this beautiful from every angle and in every light.

"Who are you important to?" I reach for the scotch, but I stop before I curve my fingers around the slender neck of the half-empty bottle.

I don't need a drink. I need a fuck.

She takes a step closer to me. The heels of her stilettos tap against the brushed oak hardwood floor. "You. Tonight."

She's right. She's also still dressed.

I cross my arms over my chest. "Take off your shoes."

Hesitation doesn't halt her. She kicks her shoes off with fanfare, sending one flying onto my Italian leather sofa.

She's no more than five-foot-three or four without the added benefit of her heels.

"The dress," I demand. "Drop the dress."

"Tit for tat." She shakes her head. "Or is it tits for that?"

I watch as her hand circles the air in front of her. "Lose the suit jacket, Dylan."

My modus operandi has remained unchanged for at least the past decade. The woman I'm with strips naked. I bring her to orgasm with my fingers, or if the temptation is strong, my mouth.

Only then do I undress and that's so I can fuck freely.

Another round might be in the cards if the first was enticing enough. Often it's not and my lover for the night will take her leave after trying to push her number on me.

I don't need phone numbers. I need space to sleep, preferably alone.

I slide my gray suit jacket from my shoulders. Folding it in half, I place it over the arm of the sofa.

"Cufflinks," she says in a voice that is a mix of a breathed whisper and a veiled moan.

Power is heady. If watching me undress gets her wet, I'll play her little game.

I remove my cufflinks, carefully placing them on the table next to the bottle of scotch.

I turn my attention back to her. Her bare feet are shifting

on the floor. It's not nervous energy. She's moving to a beat that only she can hear.

She's a natural. A born dancer, much like the woman she reminds me of.

"The dress," I repeat. "Take it off."

She shakes her head. "I'll lose the watch."

Her left hand makes quick work of the clasp on the silver watch on her right wrist. Once it's free, she tosses it at me.

I effortlessly catch it.

My gaze drops to it. It's delicate. The band is dotted with diamonds. I rest it next to my cufflinks before I place my watch beside it.

"Your turn," I point out noting that the only other jewelry she's wearing is a pair of small silver hoop earrings.

My patience should be wearing thin, but I have all night. Even though I'm aroused, this exchange is unexpected and as fascinating as the woman I'm staring at.

"No." She takes two steps closer to me. "I want you to take off your shirt."

I'd debate the point and likely win, but the white button-down shirt will be on my bedroom floor within the next thirty minutes, so I comply.

I watch her eyes as I loosen my navy blue tie before tossing it on the back of the sofa. Her gaze is riveted to my fingers. Each button that is undone reveals more of the smooth skin of my chest and my abs.

"Do you have any tattoos?" she asks, stepping closer.

The query perks my brows and my curiosity. "Is that a requirement?"

"It's a question."

I've never considered inking my skin, but that's not because I don't see the beauty of the art or believe in the meaning behind it.

The person I hate most in the world is covered with tattoos. His chest, back, and arms bore colorful ink the last time I saw him.

A tattoo on my skin would inevitably remind me of him.

I don't need or want that.

I answer the question with a push of the shirt from my shoulders.

Her eyes rake my bare torso and arms. "Turn around."

If she's this demanding in bed, a second or even third round is a given. I can't remember the last time I wanted a woman this much.

That's a lie. I can remember even though I've tried in vain to forget.

I don't move. "I'll show you my back once you show me you."

Her eyes drop to the front of her dress. It's modest, but low cut enough to reveal the promise of a pair of round tits.

She's tiny but curvy. She's exactly what I want and need tonight.

Her hands fall to the thin leather belt that is cinched around her waist. She unbuckles it before she slides it off and drops it at her feet.

My hand moves to the front of my pants. I squeeze my hardened cock through the fabric as she glides one shoulder of the dress down revealing the thin strap of a black bra.

CHAPTER THREE

*D*YLAN

I'M on her when the dress hits the floor.

My cock is throbbing inside the constraint of my pants. My heart is hammering so hard that I expect my chest to split open down the middle.

What the fuck is wrong with me?

I tug her against me, wrapping my arms around her.

The sight of those perfect tits in the black lace bra she's wearing, and the matching panties almost sent me over the edge.

The last time I shot my load in my boxer briefs I was seventeen-years-old.

That was sixteen fucking years ago.

"Kiss me," she murmurs.

I lower my mouth to hers, taking a second to run my tongue over the seam of her plump lips.

She moans into the kiss. It's not coming from a place of

need. I've heard enough of those sounds to recognize the difference between need and want.

This woman wants me just as much as I want her.

She doesn't need me, so why in the hell do I feel like I need her?

The kiss breaks when her teeth clamp down on my lower lip.

I welcome the pain. I welcome anything she gifts me with.

"Take me to bed," she demands in a whisper.

I pick her up. Her legs wrap around me. Her ankles cross at the base of my back.

I can feel the heat coming from her skin. I can sense how wet those lace panties are.

I turn us around but stop when her lips find mine again.

This time the kiss is intense and deep. Her tongue slides against mine, fighting for control.

I don't give in. I take more, wrapping my hand around the back of her head, tugging her even closer.

She sucks in a deep breath when I pull back.

Her long eyelashes bat as a smile curves her mouth. "You can kiss."

I stare into her beautiful eyes. "The bed."

"Take me there." Her lips trail a path over my jaw. "Now, Dylan."

I steal one last kiss before I take a step forward.

I stop in place.

Where the fuck is my bedroom?

I chuckle when I realize that she's kissed all sense out of me. I turn us around again.

"What's so funny?" she asks, tapping my shoulder with her fingernail.

I want those nails digging into my skin when I'm inside

of her. I want her to mark me. I want the pain to linger for days so I don't forget her.

I shake the thought away with a heavy sigh.

I always forget them.

I can't remember the name of the woman I fucked last week or the one I took to bed the week before that.

Maybe it's best that I don't know this woman's name. I fear I'd never forget it and there's only room in my memory for one name.

"Dylan?" The woman wrapped around me lures my attention with a drag of her fingernail over my shoulder and down my bicep. "Are you all right?"

I'll never be all right.

I'm fine. I'm okay. I'm put together enough that I can fuck this woman into tomorrow and leave her with a memory of a man named Dylan who gave her a night to remember.

I answer her with a hard press of my mouth to hers before I carry her down the hallway and into my bedroom.

———

ONE ROUND with her won't be enough.

She's on her back on my bed. Her light brown hair surrounds her head and shoulders like a halo.

This woman is no angel.

I'd call her the devil, but she's far from that.

She's a savior.

She was sent to save me from the hell that I've been living in for the past fifteen years.

Even if my salvation lasts only tonight, I'll fall to my knees in gratitude.

I toe out of my shoes, rip off my socks, and drop my pants.

The bulge inside my boxer briefs catches her eye immediately. I'm long and thick. The only measure that matters to me is the degree of pleasure the women I've been with have experienced.

I know I have an impressive cock. I've heard it enough times that there's no reason for humility.

I slide my boxer briefs down.

Her tongue glides over her bottom lip. At any other time, with another woman, I'd take that as an invitation.

I'd crawl onto the bed and shove my dick between a pair of eager lips, but I want my lover tonight to experience what I can do for her.

I won't be greedy with this woman.

I rest a knee on the bed and look down at her. "Undo your bra."

She nods in response. Her hands jump to the clasp at the front. She fumbles with it briefly before it lets go and her ample tits spill out.

I lower my mouth to her right nipple. Taking it between my teeth, I lick it slowly with the tip of my tongue.

Her breath catches. I sense her holding back a moan. It's there in the arch of her back and the graze of her hand over the skin of my neck.

I focus on the other breast, gliding my tongue over her soft flesh until I bite that nipple. I'm not tender this time.

"My panties," she whimpers. "Take them off."

"Take them off," I repeat back.

I want her to undress for me. Her body is a gift, and I want her to unwrap it.

She moves to slide the triangle of black lace down her legs.

I'm transfixed. I can't take my eyes away from her body.

She rubs her thighs together before her legs open. Her cunt is perfectly pink and wet.

I crave a taste. I want to lap at her until she can't form any word but my name.

Her fingers glide over her cleft. "I need you inside of me now."

I stare at her hand; at the way her delicate fingers circle her clit. I could sit here, with my dick pulsing with need and watch her get herself off.

I could, but I won't.

I move quickly, shifting on the bed until I'm facing the nightstand. I dump the box of condoms that sits in plain view. My hand grabs for one.

I rip the packet open, sheath my cock, and turn back to the sight of this gorgeous woman laid open and bare for me.

Pushing between her legs, I look down at her. "This is just the beginning. You're mine for the night."

I thrust into her. It's so hard and sudden that she cries out.

I take her in long strokes, the pace building, the raw need surfacing until the bed shakes beneath us and she comes with a moan that wraps itself around me so tightly that it drives me into an intense orgasm that steals everything from me but this moment in time with this woman.

CHAPTER FOUR

DYLAN

"MR. COLT? SIR? ARE YOU ALIVE?"

If I'm hearing those words, I sure as hell can't be dead.

I manage to crack one of my eyelids open far enough to see a stocky figure standing at the foot of my bed.

Sunlight is pouring into the room.

I never wake to sunlight.

"What?" I bark back, my hand falling to the space next to me. I slide it over the sheet but come up empty. "Where the fuck is she?"

"Who?"

Christ.

Gunner Runyan, my ever-present, annoying-as-hell assistant, is standing in my bedroom, and I'm naked.

I tug the twisted blanket around my waist.

"There's a woman here." I use sheer will to pry open both of my eyelids against the assault of light. I didn't draw the blinds before I fell asleep.

I couldn't think straight last night.

"No, sir." I don't have to look at him to know that he's shaking his head. "You were the only one here when I arrived."

"Bullshit," I mutter under my breath.

"It's not bullshit," he says in an even tone. "I can go back and check every room if you want, but I guarantee that there's no one in this apartment but you and me."

She left. She goddamn left when I was sleeping.

Gunner clears his throat as if I need a reminder that he's standing mere feet away from me.

"Why are you here?" I shield my eyes from the sunlight with my hand so I can shoot him a death stare.

He's dressed as he always is in a three-piece black suit, a white button-down shirt, and a light blue tie. Gunner doesn't give a shit if it's one hundred degrees outside. His wardrobe never changes.

His blond hair is cut short and neat. His green eyes are always keen and focused.

He may annoy me, but he's the best assistant I've ever had. His salary and perks prove that.

"I tried calling you." He motions to the nightstand. "Your phone was dead when I arrived. I'm charging it now."

I glance in the direction he's pointing. I see dozens of condom wrappers with only one opened, my phone, and an alarm clock that I never bother to set.

I wake up every single fucking day at four thirty-five without fail.

Narrowing my eyes, I spot the time on the clock.

"It's seven-thirty?" I dart into a sitting position. "Tell me it's not seven-thirty, Gunner."

His gaze drops to the gold watch on his wrist. "It's seven-thirty two according to my time. I synchronize it every morning with my computer's clock. It's accurate within a quarter of a second."

"Fuck." I swing my legs over the side of the bed, not caring if Gunner gets an eyeful of my dick.

He immediately turns his back to me. "You're due in court in less than ninety minutes. I also need to point out that you have a meeting in precisely thirteen minutes with Mrs. Jenkinson. She's aware that you can't give her more than twenty minutes of your time today."

I'd ask why the fuck I have a meeting before court, but I'm the arrogant asshole who thought I could fit that in.

I haven't reviewed my notes for the Alcester case.

I'm representing the wife. Trudy Alcester is looking to end her marriage to her cheating bastard of a husband, Troy Alcester.

He's ranked in the top five on virtually every national list there is for the wealthy and elite.

They met and married before he struck gold in the technology market. With no prenup in existence and a string of mistresses set to testify, I'll help Mrs. Alcester start a new, very comfortable life.

My only hurdles at this point are Mr. Alcester's lawyer, Kurt Sufford, and the parade of paparazzi that will be waiting on the steps of the courthouse hoping for a picture of the jilted wife or one of the three mistresses I have lined up waiting to tell their stories.

"I'll meet you back at the office?" Gunner asks, starting toward my bedroom door.

"Pick me up a coffee on your way there." I rake both hands through my hair.

Gunner stops mid-step, his back still to me. "About the woman that was here, sir. I believe she may have forgotten something. I noticed a woman's watch on the bar when I was emptying the ice bucket. Should I take it and have it returned to her?"

I have no goddamn idea who she is or why she bolted before I woke up.

We fell asleep wrapped around each other after we fucked. My intention to catch a few minutes of sleep before I screwed her again turned into a solid seven hours.

"I'll take care of the watch," I say curtly. "Get that coffee and get back to the office before Martha Jenkinson arrives."

"I'm on that."

I head to the shower as he disappears out of view.

———

I DON'T FLY BLINDLY whether it's in the bedroom or the courtroom.

I never fall asleep with a woman next to me. I'm a gentleman who sees the woman I fuck out the door and into a cab before he calls it a night.

I can't believe I drifted off last night with my lover in my arms.

I have her watch in the pocket of my navy blue suit jacket and the memory of her body stored away.

I wish to fuck I would have gotten her name.

Anyone who thinks they can wander around Manhattan anonymously is mistaken. I have a private investigator on my payroll. The man is the second coming of Sherlock Holmes. I know, without a doubt, that he could find the mystery woman with as little as her first name.

I don't even have that to offer him.

I've tried to convince myself that I want to know who she is so I can return the watch, but it reaches far beyond that.

I want her back in my bed.

Thinking about her voice, her body, and that sound she made when she came is clouding my common sense.

I'm sitting in the courtroom with Trudy Alcester by my side and a gallery filled with reporters.

I didn't have time to crack open the envelope Gunner left for me last night. I scooped it into my palm before I left my apartment, but it's sitting back on the desk in my office.

I know I've got the facts straight unless Kurt Sufford decided to pull something out of his hat before this hearing.

I haven't looked over at the table where he's sitting. I sense that Kurt and his jerk of a client both have smug grins on their faces.

I heard them arrive to a chorus of applause from the gallery. It has to be the employees of Alcester Industries that Troy pays to fill several seats in the courtroom.

He did it during the first hearing we had months ago when the judge ordered the case be sent to a mediator.

Anyone who needs to bring their own cheering section to their divorce proceedings deserves to be hung up from his balls.

"All rise," the bailiff calls out just as the clock hits nine o'clock sharp.

I stand and bow my head as he runs through his chatter about court being in session and the honorable Judge Peggy Mycella presiding over these proceedings.

I've been in Peggy's courtroom enough times to know that she won't make eye contact until she's settled behind the bench.

She reads out the docket number, combs a hand through her short blonde bob, and takes a sip of water before she asks if we're ready to proceed.

"Judge?" Kurt adds a high note to his voice. "If it so

pleases the court, I'd like a moment to speak before we get started."

I roll my eyes and glance over at my client. The look on her face is pure frustration. She wants this over with as quickly as I do.

Mediation got us nowhere so we're here, facing off with her soon-to-be ex-husband in front of a courtroom filled with reporters who are looking for any sordid tidbit they can run alongside a picture of the once happy couple.

"It would please me to get through this hearing within the hour." Judge Mycella taps her fingernails on the wooden bench. "Say what you need to say."

"I request a continuance, your honor."

That finally turns my head to the left.

I narrow my eyes at the sight that awaits me.

What the actual fuck?

The woman standing between Kurt and his client may be looking straight ahead, but I know that face. I stared at that profile in the car on the way to my apartment less than twelve hours ago.

She's not wearing the black dress she had on last night. Today she's dressed in a conservative navy blue jacket and matching skirt. Under the jacket is a white blouse. Her long hair is tied into a bun at the base of her neck.

"What the hell?" I mutter under my breath, shaking my head because I'm sure as fuck dreaming this. I have to be.

"What's wrong?" Trudy jabs an elbow into my side. "What is Troy's lawyer trying to pull?"

"A continuance?" The judge removes her eyeglasses and pops a brow. "Why, Mr. Sufford?"

"The old ticker needs a tune-up." Kurt pats the middle of his chest with his hand. "I'm having heart surgery the day after tomorrow."

"I'm genuinely sorry to hear that." The judge's gaze shifts from Kurt to me.

"My co-counsel needs time to get up to speed on the case." Kurt's arm waves in front of the woman I fucked last night.

The judge leans forward, her eyes pinned to the woman I had pinned to my bed just a few hours ago. "I haven't seen your co-counsel in my courtroom before. An introduction is in order, Mr. Sufford."

I turn my full attention to the woman I took home with me last night.

Kurt clears his throat, but her hand on his shoulder stills him.

She looks to the judge before glancing in my direction. Her eyes lock with mine. "I'm Eden Conrad, your honor."

"No fucking way," I blurt out. "There's no way in hell you're Eden Conrad."

I hear the distant thump of the judge's gavel as she calls order in the court and warns me that she'll hold me in contempt if I use that language again.

I stare at the woman I fucked last night. There's no goddamn way she's the same girl I knew in high school. That girl has haunted my thoughts constantly since I last saw her on the night I graduated.

With all hell breaking loose around me, I fall into my chair and rest my head in my hands.

Fuck my life.

CHAPTER FIVE

Dylan

"COUNSEL WILL APPROACH." Judge Mycella dips her chin. "Now."

I drag my ass off the chair without glancing to my left.

I'm stuck in some alternate reality where the sins of my past are finally catching up to me.

Kurt takes a spot next to me in front of the bench. The woman calling herself Eden Conrad stands next to him.

"What's going on, Mr. Colt?" Peggy asks tersely. "You know better than to have an outburst in my courtroom."

"My apologies." I keep my gaze on her as I adjust my light blue tie and button my suit jacket. "I need time to regroup, your honor."

"You'll get time." She looks over at Kurt and the woman next to him. "I take it you know, Mr. Colt?"

"We've met," she answers in that same soft voice she spoke in last night when she was in my apartment.

Fuck this woman. What the fuck is she doing to me?

I finally turn to look at her. "Who put you up to this?"

"Mr. Colt." My name lashes off Peggy's tongue with an unspoken warning. "What is your problem?"

"She's not Eden Conrad," I say it with conviction because there's zero chance in hell that the woman I'm looking at is the same Eden Conrad I went to high school with.

"I am Eden Conrad." She tilts her head.

"You're not that Eden Conrad," I snap back.

"That Eden Conrad?" Peggy scratches her eyebrow. "You're going to clarify what that means, Dylan."

Peggy and I travel in some of the same social circles.

She's two decades older than me, generous, and funny as hell. In the courtroom she's tough-as-nails, fair, and firm.

I've never expected a favor from her, and not one has ever been granted.

She rules by the law.

"I knew an Eden Conrad years ago." I look over at the woman claiming to be Eden. "She's not that Eden Conrad."

"In my defense, your honor..."

"You're not on trial, Ms. Conrad." Peggy smiles gently at the woman. "Is there a history here that the court needs to be aware of?"

"We went to the same high school." The woman sighs. "Mr. Colt doesn't recognize me. I've changed since the last time we saw each other."

I want to point out that we saw each other last night. The only thing that's changed is her assertion that she's Eden Conrad.

For fuck's sake, if she were Eden, she would have said something when my dick was buried inside her.

I would have known.

Christ. There's no way in hell I can be in the same room breathing the same air as Eden Conrad and not know it.

"The Eden Conrad I knew would never have pursued a law degree." I take a deep breath. "That's not who she was. You may be the same height as her and have the same eye color, but you're not her."

Kurt hasn't said a word throughout this until now. He clears his throat. "Your honor, may I say something?"

"Please." Peggy waves a hand in the air as the muted chatter from the gallery floats in the air behind us.

"You obviously weren't brought up to speed on the change of counsel." Kurt glances at me. "I mentioned it in a courtesy call to Gunner two days ago. You might want to ask your assistant why he didn't pass the message on to you."

He likely did. It was probably noted in very large bold type in that envelope he dropped off for me last night.

"Here's her bio in short form." Kurt faces me head-on. "I've known Eden since the day she was born. Her dad, Walt, and I met when we were kids. She was enrolled in the honors program in a high school in Chicago. She was all set up to go to Ohio State for dance, but had to bow out for personal reasons. She earned her degree at Harvard Law. If any of that rings a bell, you're looking at an old friend."

I reach for the edge of the bench to steady myself.

"Does that clear things up, Dylan?" Peggy taps her finger on my hand. "Is she the Eden Conrad you used to know?"

I look past Kurt's shoulder to where she's standing. I study her face. My gaze finally lands on her neck and the star-shaped sapphire pendant hanging from a thin silver chain.

She used to wear that pendant for good luck. I always thought it made the color of her eyes appear more vibrant. It still does.

"I'm the Eden Conrad he used to know," Eden says softly.

"Is there any reason why we can't proceed at the end of the month?" Peggy asks Eden.

She shakes her head. "I can't think of a reason. Can you, Dylan?"

I can think of a million reasons why I can't do this, but I can't get a word past the lump caught in my throat.

"That's settled." Peggy leans back in her chair. "We're in recess until the thirtieth. Good luck with the surgery, Kurt. I'll see you two back here in fourteen days."

———

BY THE TIME I'm out of the courtroom, Eden is gone.

A million reasons why I can't go toe-to-toe with her in court morphed into a million questions that I want to throw in her perfect goddamn face.

That face.

Once I realized I was looking at the girl I knew from high school, I saw pieces of her in the woman I fucked last night.

It's there in the mesmerizing blueness of her eyes, and the way she tilts her chin and those lips. Those beautiful full lips that have always tempted me.

Lips that I finally kissed last night.

I close my eyes against the assault of emotions.

I fucked Eden Conrad and didn't even know it.

My phone vibrates in my pocket. I watch as the elevator doors open and a group of people rushes on.

I should be one of them. Typically, I'd be halfway back to my office by now with a plan to fill the unexpected free time I have today with billable appointments.

I reach into my pocket to fish out the phone, but my fingers land on something else.

I smooth my thumb over the face of the watch that she left at my apartment. I yank it out and stare down at it.

I have no idea what the hell is going on, but there's only one person who can tell me.

It's time to return this watch to its rightful owner.

CHAPTER SIX

EDEN

I'VE BEEN in New York City less than seventy-two hours, and I've already tipped my life upside down.

I knocked Dylan Colt's life sideways.

That wasn't planned.

None of this was planned.

My mission was simple. I came to Manhattan to help Kurt. He called me asking if I would be willing to spend a few weeks in the city taking over one of his most important cases.

Kurt Sufford has always been like an uncle to me. Three years ago, he gave me a job in the Buffalo office of Sufford, Lake & Chisholm.

This is the first time he's requested I come to Manhattan to help him with a case.

"Eden?"

I glance over my shoulder to find Noelle Sufford standing in the doorway of my bedroom.

Technically, it's her second bedroom. Noelle is letting me crash in her spare room while I work on her dad's case.

I may be three years younger than her, but she's one of my closest friends.

A frown settles over her lips. "You look like you've seen a ghost. Are you okay?"

"I'm fine, Dr. Sufford," I shoot back with a smile.

I was there when Noelle graduated from medical school. At just thirty-five years old, she's working toward her goal of setting up her own practice one day.

Noelle's brother, Marcus, is one of the most respected pediatricians in Manhattan. Noelle didn't follow in his footsteps. Plastic surgery is her passion.

"I didn't expect you to be here." She tucks a piece of her red hair behind her ear. "Dad said you two had a court date today."

As soon as Judge Mycella called recess, Kurt was on his way out of the courthouse. In the Uber on the way back to the office, Kurt received a call from a potential character witness for Troy Alcester.

I offered to take the meeting.

That will happen twenty minutes from now in an apartment two blocks from here.

I misjudged the time it would take me to get across town, so I stopped in here for a refresh of my makeup and a glass of cold water.

Noelle takes a few steps closer to me. She's dressed in a pair of black pants and a short sleeve sweater that's the same shade as her green eyes.

"I'm on a break. Shouldn't you be at work?" I question with a perk of my brow.

"I came home for an early lunch today." She sighs.

Our schedules have kept us from spending much time

together in person the last few years, but we've made up for it by FaceTiming.

I know worry on my friend's face when I see it.

"You trust the doctor performing your dad's surgery, don't you?" I ask, narrowing the space between us with a few short steps.

"She's a brilliant cardiologist."

I squeeze her hand. "She'll do her job. Your dad is the most stubborn person I know. He's going to come out of this better than ever."

"When did you get to be so wise?" Her gaze narrows. "There was a time when I was the one comforting you."

Noelle never left my side during the worst time of my life.

I'll do everything in my power to help guide her through this.

"It's my turn to take care of you." I wrap my arm around her shoulder.

"I'm here for you too." She leans into me. "If you need an ear, I have two."

Telling her about what happened between Dylan and me last night would help me sort through what I'm feeling, but I need to handle this on my own.

I'm the one who went home with him and got into his bed.

Now, I have to face the consequences of not confessing that I was the girl he knew in high school.

The same girl who thought she'd never see him again.

———

TWO HOURS LATER, I step into the afternoon sunshine flooding the streets of Manhattan.

The meeting I just wrapped up couldn't have gone any smoother. I spoke to a woman who is going to take the witness stand to sing the praises of Troy Alcester. She's not my star witness, but her words will set the stage for the slam-dunk I intend to deliver before the judge makes her final decision.

When Kurt and I first sat down to go over the case, he may have neglected to mention that our opposing counsel is Dylan Colt, but he did drop a bombshell in my lap about his client.

Trudy Alcester's closet isn't just filled with designer handbags and shoes. The woman has some hidden secrets that I have every intention of uncovering.

Kurt's private investigator discovered new information two days ago. The continuance we were granted today will give me enough time to prepare a case that will level the playing field between my client and his estranged wife.

Nothing is fair in love and divorce.

I realized that during the first case I handled after I started working at Sufford, Lake & Chisholm. I watched a couple who had been together more than twenty years go at each other in a courtroom in Buffalo like two rabid animals crossing paths in a dark alleyway.

I fish my phone out of my tote bag when it starts ringing.

I answer immediately when I realize it's Kurt's assistant calling.

"Ms. Conrad? Is that you?" she asks before I say a word.

"It's me," I answer with a smile. "How are you, Mrs. Burton?"

I don't know her first name. I'm not sure Kurt does either. He told me that he's called her Mrs. Burton since he hired her more than ten years ago.

"Stressed." She lets out an exaggerated sigh. "The

attorney representing Mrs. Alcester is looking for you. He came down here shortly before noon. I told him you were out of the office. He waited around for more than thirty minutes. He's called three times since he left."

I'm not entirely surprised, although I didn't expect Dylan to make an in-person appearance at my office. "I see."

"He's persistent." She emphasizes the last syllable. "I told him I couldn't give out your cell number without your permission, regardless of how urgent he thinks the matter is."

"I appreciate you not sharing my number." I start down the sidewalk in the direction of Noelle's apartment building.

"Of course," she says curtly. "He said he had something to give you. I told him you were in a meeting and I wasn't sure when you'd be back to the office. I didn't know if you'd return at three or four or…"

"I won't be back today," I say in a rush. "I have another meeting."

"You do?" Her tone shifts from frustration to curiosity. "I have your schedule in front of me and I don't see anything."

"This is Buffalo business. I have a Skype meeting in fifteen minutes with my team back home to go over our open cases."

I resist the temptation to remind her that I told her about it this morning.

"I'll be taking that out of the office." I slow my pace. "If Mr. Colt calls again, tell him he can leave the item with you."

I glance down at my bare wrist.

I didn't realize that I left my watch at Dylan's apartment until I was getting ready for court this morning. I'd ducked out of his place after he fell asleep.

"I did suggest that." I can hear the smile in her voice. "He told me that he couldn't do that. He wants to hand whatever it is directly to you."

Dylan has always been aggravatingly persistent.

"If he calls again tell him that it's not an urgent matter and I'll see him in court next week."

"You sound as if you know what he wants to give you."

I know a lure when I hear one. Mrs. Burton is looking for some inside information. I'm not going to tell her that I left my watch in Dylan's apartment after I had sex with him.

"Please relay the message to him," I say as I wait to cross the street. "I'll be back in the office tomorrow. I'll see you then?"

"I'll be here bright and early."

Ending the call, I tap my shoe against the sidewalk as I wait for the light to change.

I expected New York to be an exciting break from my boring life in Buffalo. The city has already delivered that in spades.

CHAPTER SEVEN

*D*YLAN

"WAIT JUST A FUCKING MINUTE, COLT." Barrett Adler, my oldest and most annoying friend, spits those words out with a laugh. "Let me get this straight. You want me to drop everything so I can go home and search for a yearbook from high school?"

Glancing at my phone, I scrub my hand over the back of my neck. "I need it. Just do it."

"Find your own goddamn yearbook. I've got an afternoon of meetings ahead of me."

I fall into the chair behind my desk. "Jesus, Barrett. Did you forget that I tossed mine in the trash? I need you to courier your copy to me."

I take the phone off speaker and raise it to my ear.

"What the fuck is going on?" he asks as the sound of traffic seeps in.

He's left his office at Garent Industries in downtown Chicago. He's on the move.

"Eden Conrad," I say her name because I know. I fucking know that's all I need to say and he'll clue in.

"I don't know where the hell my yearbook is." He mutters something under his breath I can't make out. "I'll head home and search for it. It's in a box somewhere. I'll find it."

I close my eyes. "Listen, Barrett. Thanks."

"No need to thank me. You'll have it in your hands by tomorrow morning."

Ending the call, I drop my phone on my desk.

A quick knock at my office door lures my gaze up, but before I can tell whoever is on the other side to go away, I'm looking at my partner, Griffin Kent.

I point out the obvious to him. "You're supposed to wait until I say 'come in' before you open the door, asshole."

Griffin breaks into a smile. "It's nice to see you too."

"Close the door," I spit out.

He slams the door shut with a push of his foot.

The dark gray suit on his back and designer tie around his neck is expected. The ever-present grin on his face is new. It was planted there by his fiancée, Piper Ellis when she walked into the reception area of our offices and his life last year.

He scratches the side of his nose. "Are you sick?"

I know where he's going with this so I skip past the list of annoying questions that he's about to ask and I get to the meat of the matter. "Do I need to be ill for my partner to lend me a helping hand?"

I had Gunner direct all my work-related calls to Griffin this afternoon. I also instructed him to send a drop-in appointment Griffin's way even though it was with a prospective client that I've been trying to charm for the past month.

Griffin and I met in college. We propped each other up through law school,

It's been hard work to get to the point we are at today, but we did it side-by-side through the good times and the bullshit.

I trust Griffin almost as much as I trust Barrett. The big difference is that Griffin knows the bare basics about my past with Eden. Barrett lived through it with me.

"I'll always pitch in when you need me to." He settles on one of the leather guest chairs in front of my desk. "Seeing as how this is the first time you've ever had Gunner send a prospective client my way, I'm curious. What's going on?"

I can tell him about Eden now or wait until he looks over the Alcester case file and spots her name himself.

We back each other at every turn. It's not uncommon for me to cover a call or a meeting on one of his cases if he's tied up. He's done the same for me.

"Kurt Sufford is having heart surgery."

I start there because it's a far cry from confessing that I'm going head-to-head with Eden in the courtroom.

"You're pushing your work at me because of him?" His blue eyes study my face. "I had no idea that you two were close."

My lips curve into a smile. "You're an ass."

He shoots me a toothy grin. "You're hiding something. Spit it out, Dylan. What's happening with the Alcester case? Do you need my help?"

Handing the case over to him would be the easy way out, but I don't do easy, or simple. Challenge is what gets me out of bed in the morning.

I can handle the case. Shit, I can even handle Eden in the courtroom.

What I can't handle is that I fucked her last night, and I felt something more than a satisfying orgasm.

"Kurt brought his co-counsel to court this morning." I lean back in my chair. "You're not going to believe who it is."

"It's not Darren Macon, is it? That guy is a weasel. I swear to God he lied to the judge's face during the Campbell trial. I almost lost that case because of his bullshit."

"It's Eden Conrad."

His eyes narrow. "Say again."

"Eden Conrad is representing Troy Alcester from here on." I tap my fingers on my desk.

"The Eden Conrad you went to high school with?" he questions. "How the fuck is that even possible?"

"You tell me," I say jokingly with an exaggerated chuckle. "Apparently, she's a lawyer and Troy Alcester is her client."

Griffin bolts to his feet. "I'm taking over the case."

I follow suit, rising from my chair. "Like hell you are. I've got this."

His arms cross his chest. "I know enough about your past with this woman to see that this is a disaster in the making. We owe it to Trudy Alcester to give her our best."

"I am our best," I point out. "I'll see this through to the end."

"When's your next court date?" He glances down at his watch. "I'll get Joyce to work her magic so I'm available for that."

Joyce, Griffin's assistant, is a miracle worker, but her time is better spent keeping his current cases in order.

"I've got this, Griffin," I stress again.

He rakes a hand through his brown hair, anxiety dictating his movements. "Have you two talked outside of the courtroom?"

Telling Griffin that I took Eden to bed last night serves no purpose, so I keep that information to myself.

"You need to put the past to rest with this woman." He

drops into responsible partner mode. "It's best for the Alcester case."

I'll win the case regardless of what is happening between Eden and me.

"I'm down the hall if you need anything." He manages a half-smile. Worry is knitting his brow.

I offer the only words I can think of to reassure him that I won't let my past with Eden impact the firm's reputation. "I have a solid case. Trudy Alcester is going to come out of this a very wealthy and happy woman."

"That's the end goal," he says with conviction. "Get the job done and I'll buy you a beer to celebrate."

I toss him a curt nod.

I'll get the job done. Eden Conrad may have owned me last night, but she doesn't stand a chance against me in the courtroom.

CHAPTER EIGHT

Eden

"DID Eden tell you that she saw an old friend in court today?" Kurt grins from ear-to-ear. A small piece of broccoli stuck between his two front top teeth is a beacon I can't take my eyes off of.

If I had known that Kurt and his wife, Thelma, were coming to dinner tonight, I would have found an excuse to be out.

Not that I have anywhere to go in Manhattan, but I feel like I'm intruding on Sufford family time. Given the gravity of the surgery that Kurt is going to endure in less than two days, I feel guilty for taking any of his attention away from his wife and daughter.

"She didn't," Noelle answers with a lilt in her voice. "Who did you see, Eden?"

"Someone from high school." I shrug it off like it's no big deal, even though seeing Dylan in court this morning was jarring.

Having sex with him last night rocked me to my core, but no one sitting here has any idea that I went home with the man.

"He's more than someone," Kurt mocks my voice. He tosses me a wink before he continues, "Dylan Colt is his name. He's the second best divorce attorney in this city."

"Who's the first?" I joke with a wink of my own in Kurt's direction.

Kurt waves a finger at me. "That's the sassiness I expect from you in the courtroom. Going up against Dylan Colt isn't an easy task, but I sense you have an advantage that I never had."

I clench my jaw to keep my mouth from falling open.

Dylan used to boast about his conquests in high school. I pray that he's matured since then and has stopped telling anyone who will listen to him who he took to bed.

"What advantage does Eden have?" Noelle smirks.

"I've never seen Dylan so rattled before." Kurt cuts into a piece of the roasted chicken breast that Noelle prepared. "He looked about ready to faint when he realized that Eden went to high school with him."

Before Noelle can ask another question, I attempt to steer the conversation in a different direction. "I'm feeling great about the case. I had a meeting this afternoon that I think will help us."

"I knew it would." Kurt shoves a forkful of mashed potatoes into his mouth.

"So you and Dylan were friends?" Noelle reaches for her water glass. "You never mentioned him to me."

During the weeks following graduation, Noelle met a handful of my friends from school. Dylan was off backpacking in Europe.

"Let's not talk about that right now. Tonight is about

family, not work." Thelma says, picking up her water glass and holding it in the air. "Here's to a happy and healthy future."

I glance over at Kurt. He can't take his eyes off the woman he married almost forty years ago.

"To the future." Noelle raises her glass too.

Kurt and I follow in a toast to tomorrow and every day to come.

NOELLE TURNS the lock on the door of her apartment and spins to face me. "Tell me more about Dylan Colt."

I could tell that she was curious when she cornered me in the kitchen after dinner to ask about Dylan. I avoided answering by focusing all of my attention on the dishes.

I loaded the dishwasher and scrubbed down the counters and the sink. I was just about to roll up the sleeves of my white sweater to start cleaning the oven when her parents announced that they had to take off.

I gave them both a hug and a wave as they walked out the door to make their way back to their apartment on the Upper East Side.

"We went to high school together back in Chicago." I try to change the subject again. "Where did you get those jeans?"

Noelle glances down at the faded, ripped jeans she's wearing before she points at me. "Wherever you got your jeans. We're wearing the same brand and style."

Dammit.

I should have complimented the floral blouse she's wearing.

"You blushed when my dad said Dylan's name."

I rest a hand on my hip. "It was my first time in a

Manhattan courtroom and we had a sidebar over the fact that Dylan didn't recognize me. I said my name. He said I wasn't the Eden Conrad he used to know and…"

"Oh, shit." Noelle rushes to me. "Eden, I'm sorry."

I let her take me in her arms for a hug.

She leans back and studies my face. "I think you look even more beautiful now than you did in high school."

I've lost track of how many times she's said those words to me since I was seventeen. I reply the same way I always do, "You're the best."

"I know it's hard when you see someone from your past." A sigh escapes her. "I'm a call away if you ever need me."

"I'll keep that in mind."

Her gaze drops to the watch on her wrist. "I have to be at work before dawn. I need some sleep."

I need sleep too, but it won't find me. I can't quiet my mind. It's not the Alcester case that's consuming me. It's Dylan.

I know he didn't show up at my office today just to return the watch. He wants answers. I'm the only one who can give them to him since I'm the woman who crawled into his bed and his arms without telling him that I was the Eden he walked away from on the night we graduated. It was the night that changed the course of my life forever.

CHAPTER NINE

DYLAN

"I'M ALL for helping out an old friend, but this is bullshit."
Barrett slaps my shoulder. "My flight was delayed for two
hours. Do you have any idea what time it is?"

It's just past one in the morning.

I've been pacing the floors of my apartment since he
texted me from O'Hare International to tell me that he was
hand delivering our senior yearbook.

"I owe you." I take a step back and look him over.

I make it a point to see Barrett at least a few times a year.
That typically happens when I venture back to my hometown
to visit my parents and their significant others.

I time those visits so they don't coincide with any major
holidays or events.

My family is manageable in small doses. I don't need the
pressure of being thrown headfirst into a reunion with
cousins, aunts, and uncles I haven't seen in more than a
decade.

Beers with Barrett make my time back in Chicago more bearable.

"You can start paying me back by inviting me in." His blue eyes survey the room behind me. "I see you've done nothing with the place since the last time I was here."

I step to the side to let him pass.

He slides the handle of the duffel bag that's slung over his shoulder down before he drops it at my feet.

"I'm taking the bedroom without the view." He stretches both arms. "I'm beat. If I give you the goods, can I hit the sack?"

Judging by the way he's dressed, he didn't make time for a change of clothes before he went to the airport. He's still dressed in a tailored gray suit, a button-down shirt, and a tie.

Jeans and T-shirts are his usual attire when he shows up here for a rare weekend trip.

I'm wearing the Yankees T-shirt and dark sweatpants I put on after my second shower. I took the first when I got home from work, but restlessness set in while I waited for him, so I went for a run.

The evening heat bore down on me, so another shower was in order.

"Where's the yearbook?" I eye the bag on the floor.

"It's on top." He points to the zipper. "Now is as good as time as any to explain why the fuck you wanted it, Colt."

My hands are on the duffel bag before the words leave his mouth. I tug the zipper open and wrench out the yearbook.

I flip through the pages as Barrett crosses the room to my home bar.

I took a small shot of scotch over an hour ago in an effort to calm the hell down.

It didn't work.

Barrett pours himself two fingers, not bothering to ask if I want the same. He sees my empty glass. He knows I've had my fill.

"You mentioned Eden on the phone." He turns to look at me. "You sounded shook up. That's why I'm here."

I don't glance up at him because I'm still trying to locate the page in the yearbook that holds the answer to at least one of the questions that's been nagging at me all fucking day.

"She's in New York." Looking up, I try to keep my voice at an even tone. "I saw her yesterday and again today."

That brings the glass to his lips again. The scotch disappears in one gulp. "Eden Conrad is here? What the hell is she doing in New York?"

"She's a lawyer."

"A lawyer? You're not serious, are you?"

My gaze skims the open page in front of me. I scan the pictures of the seniors finally landing on the face of the woman I thought I'd never forget.

I see it now.

Christ, why didn't I see it in the club or when I had her in my bed?

She's changed, but it's her.

I slam the yearbook shut. "Jesus, what the fuck is wrong with me?"

I stalk to the bar and half fill the glass I used earlier. I take a mouthful of scotch and swallow.

"Is that rhetorical or are you waiting for me to answer that?" Barrett sets his glass down. "You're torn up from seeing her after all these years. Is that what's happening here or is this emotional shit storm I'm witnessing something else?"

I finish off the scotch, slam the glass down so hard it shatters, and I turn to face him. "I fucked her. I fucked Eden

Conrad last night, and I didn't have a goddamn clue it was her."

———

BARRETT HANDS me a mug of coffee.

I needed the coffee as much as he needed the time it took to brew it to process what I said.

He stared at me after I confessed that I took Eden to bed without realizing who she was.

Fuck.

All these years. All the want and I treat her like every other woman I've screwed.

Jesus, I'm an asshole. I'm nothing but a selfish asshole.

I've used women for years in search of a connection I could never find until last night.

Even if I wanted to make amends to the hundreds of women I've bedded in the past fifteen years, I wouldn't know where to start. I only remember the names of a handful of them.

"So you didn't know she was Eden." Barrett shrugs out of his suit jacket. "Let's start there."

"No, let's get to the part where she shows up in court to defend my client's asshole of a husband." I put the mug on the coffee table in front of me, so it doesn't fall victim to the same fate as the glass tumbler.

"Back up the bus." He settles into a chair across from me. "Lay out what happened here, Colt, because you're all over the place and without a roadmap, I'm lost."

I scrub the back of my neck with my hand. "I went to Veil East last night to blow off some steam before my court date this morning."

"You went to the club you always go to so you could find

a woman to fuck who looks like Eden." He cocks a brow. "Don't deny it. Every woman you've been with since high school looks like her."

"I have a type," I spit back.

"You brought her home and what?"

I raise both brows. "What the hell do you think happened?"

"I think that she didn't tell you that she was Eden and you're pissed."

I am pissed. I'm confused. I'm fucking embarrassed that I didn't see it her face, or hear it in her voice.

Both have changed since high school, but the pressing need inside of me to have her was different than the other women I've been with.

Kissing her was different.

Fucking her was so different.

I should have known.

"I fell asleep, she left, and I saw her in court this morning. That's when she announced to everyone there that she was Eden Conrad." I rake both hands through my hair. "I damn near passed out."

Barrett lets out a deep laugh. "I would have paid money to see the look on your face."

"Is there a chance in hell that she didn't know who I was?" The question may sound arrogant, but I'm grasping for understanding here and I'm willing to consider every possibility.

"Maybe you weren't worth remembering." He loosens his tie. "Who the hell knows why she didn't tell you her name."

"Why didn't I know it was her?" I ask the question, as much to myself as to him.

"You've been looking for her in so many faces over so many years, that you lost sight of her." He takes a sip from the coffee mug in his hand. "Besides, how the hell could you have known she was in New York? The last we heard she was in Ohio. That's the last we heard, right?"

He's asking if I've tracked her since high school.

I have.

I Googled her name for years hoping to find a social media profile or a recent image, but I always came up empty.

The last time either of us saw Eden was at the house of one of our classmates. His parents gave him the green light for a graduation celebration for the entire senior class. We left for the airport just as the party was winding down. Exploring Europe ate up the next two months of our lives before we landed back in Chicago to go our separate ways for college.

Barrett headed west to the University of Southern California. NYU brought me east. Once I had a taste of the city, I knew it was home.

"That's the last we heard," I confirm with a nod.

"Let's look at the bright side here, Colt. I know you're thinking the same thing I am."

I study his face. "What the fuck am I thinking, Barrett?"

"You're thinking that Eden Conrad doesn't blame you for what happened fifteen years ago. If she did, she sure as hell wouldn't have come home with you."

I don't know what the hell I'm thinking.

He stands. "I'm beat. We'll pick this up tomorrow but one last thing."

I follow suit and slide up to my feet. "What?"

"Forgive yourself." He pats the center of my chest. "She's obviously thriving if she's set to beat your ass in court. Let the past go. It's time."

I manage a smile. "Who said she was going to beat my ass in court?"

"You couldn't keep it together after sleeping with her, so

you've got no chance of coming out of this with a win for your client."

"I'll win."

He laughs. "Eden's still got you wrapped around her pretty little finger, maybe now she'll finally realize it."

CHAPTER TEN

EDEN

JUST THREE MORE PEOPLE.

When I got to Palla on Fifth ten minutes ago, more than a dozen people were already in line. If my calculations are correct, I should be at the counter in the next four to six minutes depending on how many coffees or teas the people in front of me order.

Back in Buffalo, I make my coffee at my apartment, pour it into a travel mug, and walk to work every morning.

My Manhattan routine is different since the smell of coffee makes Noelle nauseous.

I glance down at my phone. I'm supposed to be at my office in the next twenty minutes although Kurt made it clear that I can set my own schedule as long as I get my work done. I'm only a block away so as long as no one in front of me orders a dozen coffees, I'll make it there on time.

The brown-haired woman in front of me glances over her

shoulder and smiles. "If I had saved every dollar I spent here, I would be retired by now."

At home, I'm the first to engage in idle conversation with people. Two weeks ago at the grocery store a woman asked if I knew how to tell if a pineapple is ripe. Thirty minutes after she asked the question, I was helping her take her groceries to her car while she bounced her toddler on her hip. We met for lunch a few days later.

You never know when you're going to run into a stranger who will become a friend.

"I take it you've been coming here for at least a week?"

A laugh escapes her. "I was here the day they opened, and I've been here almost every day since."

"This is my first time," I confess as the line edges forward.

"Prepared to become addicted." She winks. "If you're taking recommendations, add a blueberry scone to your order. The second you bite into it, you'll know why I told you to get one."

"How can I resist?" I take another step forward as she does.

"I'm Sadie." She turns completely around.

She's wearing a light blue dress that's tied at the waist with a white belt. A hospital badge hangs from a lanyard around her neck.

Dr. Sadie Reynolds.

"I'm Eden." I point at her badge. "My friend works out of the same hospital as you."

Her brows pop. "What's your friend's name?"

"Noelle Sufford. Dr. Noelle Sufford."

The prettier half of the Sufford siblings." She glances over her shoulder toward the counter. "I know Noelle and her brother."

Manhattan suddenly feels a little smaller to me. I can't help but smile.

"You're killing the corporate look." She points at the white pants, white blouse, and dark blue blazer I'm wearing. "What do you do?"

"She's a lawyer."

I close my eyes briefly at the sound of that voice. That smooth, seductive voice swept over me in the club the other night. I used to think Dylan's voice was deep in high school, but it has a rasp to it now that sends a charge through me.

When I open my eyes, Sadie's gaze is fixed behind me. "I take it you know him?"

I nod. "He's a lawyer too."

"Next. Who is next?" One of the baristas calls out.

"It's my turn." Sadie glances back at the counter. "It was good to meet you, Eden. I'm sure I'll see you here again."

I smile in response before she turns to approach the barista.

"Turn around, Eden."

"I'm just here to get a coffee."

"Eden, turn around." His tone is clipped.

There's no way I'm going to get out of this café without looking at Dylan, so I spin on my heel.

My gaze volleys between his ridiculously handsome face and the man standing next to him.

The blasts from the past keep coming. Seeing these two side-by-side takes me back to senior year.

"You remember Barrett Adler, don't you?" Dylan gestures to his best friend from high school.

Barrett's gaze travels over my face. He's looking for a glimpse of the shy, smart girl he used to tease.

"I remember Barrett," I shoot back.

He's as tall as Dylan. They both hover around the six-foot-three mark. Barrett's hair is dark brown. His eyes are a deeper shade of blue than Dylan's.

I'd know him anywhere.

I'm tempted to ask if he works with Dylan, but his attire suggests otherwise. Barrett is dressed in a black V-neck T-shirt and jeans. The expensive dress shoes on his feet are misplaced, but the rest of his look is casual.

Dylan is the polar opposite. Today he's wearing a dark gray suit, a white shirt, and a patterned blue tie.

He smells as expensive as he looks.

His cologne reminds me of his bed and how it felt to be there with him.

"Next." The barista calls out again. "Ma'am, you're next."

"I need to go," I glance at Dylan before my gaze lands on Barrett's face.

He's the lesser of two evils. I don't have to face him in a courtroom later this month, and he's not going to ask me to explain why I didn't say anything at the club.

"It was good to see you again, Eden." Barrett shoves a hand at me.

I hesitate before I reach for it. I don't offer the same kind words back. Instead, I ask a question that I'm not sure I want to know the answer to. "Do you two come to this coffee shop often?"

Dropping my hand, Barrett laughs. "Not a chance. I still call Chicago home. I'm heading back there this afternoon."

"I'm here every morning before work." Dylan steps closer to me. "I live on this block."

I wait for him to point out that I know that, but he falls silent.

I assumed that he'd be at his office by now, so I thought grabbing a cup of coffee here was safe.

I was wrong.

"Next." Impatience taints the barista's cheery tone. "Ma'am, your order please."

"Have a safe trip back home, Barrett," I say before I spin around.

Sucking in a deep breath, I move to the counter and order the largest coffee they have and two blueberry scones. I have a sinking feeling that I'm going to need all the help I can find to get me through today.

CHAPTER ELEVEN

DYLAN

I'M NOT arrogant enough to think Eden walked into this coffee shop with the hope that I'd stop in before work.

Kurt's office is a block over on Lexington. I see his staff here regularly, including the man himself.

It was purely coincidence that we ended up here at the same time.

Typically, I'm in my office before seven. The clock is approaching nine, but Barrett's in town, so work can wait.

I take a seat at an empty table by the window. Barrett offered to grab two coffees after Eden took off. I don't know if he thought I was going to give chase as she pushed her way through the crowded café to the exit.

This isn't the time or the place to corner her.

Barrett places a large cup in front of me before he takes the seat across the table. "Eden looks great."

I take a sip of the black coffee. It's potent. I look forward to the jolt of caffeine it offers.

Barrett went to sleep after his second glass of scotch last night. I stayed up staring at the yearbook picture of Eden.

Jesus, she was such an angel back then.

Pure and innocent. Smart and kind.

I used her to hurt someone else, never considering the toll that my actions would have.

"I can't believe she's a lawyer." He rests his back against the wooden chair. "She was smart enough to get it done. She skipped ahead a grade, didn't she?"

"In middle school," I say with a sharp nod.

It was never what Eden wanted. We met during sophomore year when she transferred to the honors program in our school. She felt out of place. She was out of place. She was too good for all of us.

"I didn't see a ring on her finger." Barrett glances at two women who pass our table. "Has she mentioned Clark at all?"

Fifteen years have passed, but the sound of that name still makes my fist clench.

Clark Dodson symbolizes everything I hate in this world.

He was the quarterback of the rival high school's football team, the dick every girl wanted, and the reason Eden planned to go to Ohio State instead of coming to New York to study at Juilliard.

Barrett's phone buzzes in the pocket of his jeans. He fishes it out while I take another sip of coffee. I don't want to discuss Clark. I try to forget he exists most of the time. I would have taken that same approach in high school, but the bastard was in my face all the fucking time.

"I need to make a few calls." Barrett skims his finger over the screen of his phone. "I won't be able to walk you to your office. I'm a shitty date."

"You're a busy COO." I chuckle. "Thanks again for the yearbook."

"There are things I need to say... want to say about Eden." He ignores the string of chimes coming from his phone. "I can tell that you're not ready to talk about it. I get it. If or when you are, I'll hop back on a plane."

"I need to figure some things out."

"It's not my place to say this, but you know I don't give a shit about my place. You need to hear this one thing."

I laugh. "Say what you need to say."

"You can't change the past, so stop looking back."

"I fucked up her life." I squint at him. "She's got to be pissed about that."

"She didn't look at you like she's pissed." He glances at his ringing phone before he sets his gaze back on me. "I didn't see any of that in her expression."

"You figured all of that out after seeing her for less than a minute?"

He holds up a hand in surrender. "I'm not an expert on all things Eden Conrad, but I like to believe I have some insight when it comes to women. She wouldn't have gotten into bed with you if she were holding a grudge or if she hated you."

"Hate sex is a thing."

His lips curve into a grin. "That I'm an expert on."

I laugh aloud.

"Look." He taps his palm on the edge of the table. "You have no idea what the past fifteen years of Eden's life look like. You let her down one night of her life. It's time to stop beating yourself up over it, because it sure as hell seems like she's doing just fine."

He means well, but even though Barrett is my oldest and closest friend, I've never told him every detail about the night of our graduation party. He has no clue that I made a decision that night that has impacted Eden's life to this day.

Only one other person on this earth knows what the fuck I did that night.

Clark Dodson, Eden's first boyfriend and the guy she wanted to marry, knows my dirty little secret.

———

I EXIT THE CAFÉ, my hand hovering over the screen of my smartphone. My contact list is open, and it would take only one touch for me to call Tony Girano.

Tony's the private investigator I keep on retainer. I run the man ragged, but he's not complaining.

The apartment he purchased in Murray Hill two years ago was financed primarily by the monthly checks I place in his hand. In exchange, he brings me concrete proof that the soon-to-be exes of my clients haven't lived up to their vows to love, honor, and cherish. Remaining faithful is something too many people struggle with much to my benefit.

I've been entertaining the idea of using Tony to bring me up to speed on where the hell Clark Dodson is and whether he's a factor in Eden's life.

I've resisted the urge until now because I didn't want confirmation that he was living the dream with Eden and a couple of kids who looked like her by his side.

Eden made it clear to me on the last night of high school that Clark was her future.

I pocket my phone, praying with everything I am that he's part of her past and that my secret remains there too.

CHAPTER TWELVE

Eden

WELL, damn.

I thought when the clock struck six and my workday ended that I'd avoided Dylan Colt's questions for the day.

Maybe it was naïve of me to believe that he wanted to focus on the case at hand since he had a courier drop off my watch earlier.

It was polished and tucked inside a rectangular white gift box.

There wasn't a card. The courier had nothing to offer but a smile and a wave of his hand when I tried to give him twenty dollars for his trouble.

He told me that Mr. Colt had taken care of it.

It seemed too good to be true, and now I know why.

Dylan Colt, looking like sex in a suit, is waiting for me on the sidewalk outside of my office. I thought he was gorgeous when he was eighteen. That lanky, messy-haired quarterback had nothing on this square-jawed, tall, breathtakingly handsome man.

"Eden." My name flies off his perfect lips as I approach him. "I see you got your watch back."

His eyes graze my arms.

I took off my blazer when I was in the elevator since it's almost ninety degrees outside. My sleeveless blouse isn't sheer, but it's thin enough that I know he can see the lace of my white bra underneath it.

It hardly matters at this point.

The man sucked on my nipples. He knows exactly what my breasts look like.

"We're having a drink together."

I raise a brow at that declaration. "No, we're not."

"We are." He flashes me one of his dimpled smiles.

My core clenches in need.

Traitor. My body is a traitor.

"I'm prepared to offer your client a deal if she'll sign off on the terms of the settlement that Kurt proposed in mediation," I say, clinging tightly to the hope that his drink invitation is business related.

"I'm going to ignore everything you just said because we both know that my client has suffered immeasurably because your client can't keep his dick in his pants."

"Your client's vagina isn't as innocent as you think it is," I blurt back.

That draws the attention of a gray-haired couple passing us on the sidewalk.

Dylan glances at them. "We're lawyers. Ignore us."

The woman gifts him with a bright smile. "It's hard to ignore you."

With a scowl on his face, her husband grabs her hand, tugging her forward.

"Have a drink with me, Eden." Dylan gestures down the street. "We need to talk, and not about the Alcesters."

He's right. We do need to talk.

"I have dinner plans at seven, so one quick drink."

His brows draw together in curiosity. I don't need to tell him that my dinner plans consist of take-out and three hours of binge-watching my favorite show.

Noelle is hanging out at her parents' apartment tonight since Kurt needs to be at the hospital at six a.m. tomorrow to be prepped for the surgery.

His gaze falls to his watch. "I can work with that. There's a place a block over. We can walk there."

I fall in step beside him, being careful not to let my hand brush against his.

I wouldn't have slept with him if I had known that he would be my archenemy in court. I can't make the mistake of touching him again.

———

DYLAN WATCHES as I take a tentative sip of the drink I ordered. I close my eyes briefly in appreciation of the skill of the bartender.

"The look on your face makes me wish that I'd ordered a Negroni instead of scotch."

"It's delicious." I chuckle. "Scotch is your go-to drink, isn't it?"

He swallows a mouthful of the amber liquid. "Guilty as charged."

I'd take that as an invitation to wade back into the Alcester case, but he made it clear that this impromptu meeting isn't about work.

"When did you decide to become a lawyer?" I ask, expecting that he'll bounce the question right back at me.

"When my folks divorced." He lifts the glass in the air. "When did you decide to withhold your identity from me?"

"Dylan." His name comes out in a whisper.

He leans his elbows on the table, narrowing the space between us. "Eden. When did you realize it was me?"

"About the same time you didn't realize I was me." I take a sip of my drink.

The corners of his lips curve up. "Touché."

I draw in a deep breath. "When you said your name was Dylan, it took me back to that quarterback in high school that I tutored. That's when I really looked at you. When we danced, I knew."

His gaze travels over my face. "Help me understand why you didn't just come out and say who you were."

I let out a heavy sigh. "I thought at some point you'd recognize me. By the time we got back to your place, the window to tell you had closed."

"That window was wide open." He curves his hand around the glass in front of him. "You should have told me who you were. I wish I would have known it was you before we fucked."

Hearing the word come out of him in a growl sets me on fire.

"Would we have fucked, Dylan?"

His brow furrows. "What?"

I push my glass aside. "If I would have told you that I was the shy nerd who tutored you in high school, do you think we would have left the club together?"

He sits in silence, his eyes trained on mine.

"I didn't set out to deceive you," I go on, my hands shaking. "I thought that we'd sleep together, I'd leave your place before you woke up, and we'd never see each other again. I didn't think you'd ever realize that I was the woman you went to high school with."

"Eden." He exhales roughly. "Eden, look…"

"You didn't remember me." Managing a small smile, I shake my head. "Or you didn't recognize me. I don't blame you for that. I know that I've changed."

It's the elephant in the room that neither of us has acknowledged.

I have no idea if Dylan even knows what happened to me on the night we graduated.

He left the party we were at to go to the airport with Barrett so they could fly to Europe for a two-month long backpacking adventure.

I never heard from him again until I saw him at the club a few nights ago.

He takes a long swallow of his drink. Placing the glass back down, he studies me carefully. "We've all changed."

"Not as much as me." I drag a fingertip over my nose and down my cheek. "I was in an accident."

He nods. "Barrett's mom told us. She said you broke your ankle."

"Both legs and my left shoulder." I fold my hands in my lap. "I wasn't wearing a seatbelt."

His eyes close briefly before they lock with mine. "Jesus, Eden."

"I hit the dashboard." A sigh escapes me. I've told the story countless times, but it never gets easier. "I was told by a doctor in the ER that my head hit the dashboard. The force of the impact shattered most of the bones in my face. That's why I don't look exactly like the Eden you knew."

CHAPTER THIRTEEN

DYLAN

THE REMAINING scotch in my glass isn't enough to crush the onslaught of emotions that hit me with the force of a hurricane.

I scrub a hand over my face.

I thought it was a broken ankle. It was so much worse.

I'd bet everything I have that she has no idea that I'm the cause of that suffering.

If she had a clue, she wouldn't be sitting here sharing a drink with me. I cost her the chance to pursue a future in professional dance. I may have cost her more.

"Dylan?" Her voice lures my gaze back to her. "I just wanted you to know why my nose looks different, and my chin. It's because of the accident."

It's because of me.

I was supposed to drive her home that night. I made that promise to her dad, but my arrogant immaturity got in the way, so she got in a car with her boyfriend.

"You still look like you," I point out.

Her full lips tug up into a smile. "I know I do, but maybe I look different enough that you didn't recognize me."

"You know that's bullshit." I chuckle. "I looked at your yearbook photo earlier. You haven't changed that much."

"Earlier as in today?" Her brows peak with interest. "You were looking at the yearbook today?"

"For the first time since we graduated." I lean back in my chair.

"I haven't looked at mine." Her voice softens. "I don't look at pictures from that long ago."

From before the accident.

Barrett first got word of the car wreck when he called home to tell his mom that we'd landed safely in Paris. She didn't have any details beyond news of Eden's broken ankle and Clark's busted arm.

I called Eden's dad, my high school football coach. I expected his rage because I hadn't followed through with my promise to watch out for his daughter and see her home safely that night.

I didn't get rage. I got silence.

He never called me back, and I never faulted him for that.

I let him down. Given everything he had done for me, it was unforgivable.

I sure as hell have never forgiven myself.

"I took us off topic." She lets out a deep and exaggerated sigh. "I should have told you who I was when we were dancing."

She should have, but she didn't.

"I don't know what came over me." Her hand darts to her chin. "I got caught up in the moment."

I glance at the bartender, but her attention is laser focused on a guy sitting in front of her at the bar.

"Can we put it behind us?" Hope edges her words. "The Alcester case is important to Kurt and I promised him I'd do right by his client... our client."

"Your client doesn't deserve you."

"My client has faults, but he's a good man," she says with conviction.

"Your client is a cheating coward." The words spill out of me without any thought.

Christ. I need to temper myself around her. Eden is not like every other attorney I go up against.

I know her heart. She's compassionate and caring. She was that one soul in high school who would befriend the kid nobody wanted anything to do with.

She rescued injured cats and worked at a homeless shelter on the weekends.

She's everything I'll never be.

She leans her elbows on the table. "You don't know your client as well as you think you do."

I scratch my chin. That lures her gaze to the light beard that covers my jaw.

"She's not perfect, Dylan." Her finger taps the table between us.

"You're itching to say something, counselor." I pat my chest. "I'm dying to hear what you think you know about my client that I don't know."

"You want me to hand my advantage over to you?" She pushes back in her chair. "That's not going to happen."

Seeing Eden like this is new for me. I like it. My cock fucking loves it. I'm hard as stone.

"Give me a hint." I smirk, because I know she's got nothing.

Trudy Alcester is almost as good of a person as Eden is. She's a philanthropist, a faithful wife, and a devoted mother.

One of her husband's mistresses blindsided her with a visit to their doorstep to expose his sins.

I got a call from Trudy the next day.

Eden's gaze darts around the bar. "Just between the two of us, when you saw me at Veil East the other night, I was there looking for someone who knows your client."

I can't contain a hearty laugh. "Who the hell in that club would know Trudy Alcester?"

She shrugs her shoulders. "You're just going to have to wait until I call that witness to the stand."

What the fuck is this? A bluff?

I had Trudy swear on everything dear to her that she wasn't hiding anything from me. I trust her, but what sorcery is Eden trying to pull.

"She hasn't fucked around." I motion for the bartender to bring me another scotch, but she can't take her eyes off the guy she's flirting with.

My phone pings in my jacket pocket just as Eden's starts ringing in her purse.

"Duty calls," she quips as she fishes in her bag.

I slide my phone out and glance down at the text on the screen.

Gunner wants a minute of my time to go over a case that we're closing out this week.

He can wait.

Apparently, Eden's client can't.

I listen as she answers the phone in a cheery tone. "Troy? How are you?"

She rises to her feet, tossing me a wave as she points at her watch.

Chatting to the bastard about their next meeting, she turns to walk away.

Some of my questions were answered tonight, but not all.

I'll get Eden alone again before week's end and when I do, business will be the last thing on my mind.

CHAPTER FOURTEEN

*E*DEN

I HAD a feeling Dylan would show up here.

I'm back at Veil East. Part of the reason is my ongoing search for a witness for the Alcester case. The other part is the music and the dance floor.

Back in Buffalo, I have a regular club that I go to when I want to blow off some steam.

I can have a drink, dance, and socialize with the people I work with in a safe environment.

Dancing is fuel for my soul.

The car accident derailed my plan to earn a living dancing, but I never lost my passion for it.

Dylan tosses me a wave from the stool he's set himself on near the bar.

I wave back, trying not to stare.

He's wearing gray slacks and a black V-neck sweater. A few strands of his hair are brushing his forehead.

It's ridiculous how gorgeous the man is.

He called the office earlier today to check on Kurt. He spoke to Mrs. Burton. She relayed the good news. Kurt's surgery this morning was a success. He'll be home early next week and back at work within the month.

I invited Noelle to come with me tonight to celebrate, but she chose sleep over dance.

I can't blame her. I saw the weariness in her eyes when I got home from work today. Relief washed over her expression when she blurted out that her dad was awake and alert enough to ask for a cheeseburger with extra bacon.

"Red is your color."

I turn my head to find a man next to me. He's blond, cute, and definitely younger than me.

"You think?" I spin in a circle to show off the wrap dress I love to wear when I'm dancing.

"I know." He flashes me a devilish grin. "You're beautiful."

I'm tempted to look over at Dylan, but I don't owe him a thing.

We share a platonic past and a one-night stand.

I wasn't his first. I know I won't be his last.

For all I know, he's already mid-pick-up tonight.

"I'm Hank." The blond man in the black suit and tie offers a hand to me. "What's your name?"

I'd ask him if it matters, but I think to him it might.

He can't be more than twenty-four or twenty-five. He took time and care with his appearance.

His jaw is closely shaved, his hair neatly trimmed, and the cologne he's wearing is expensive. At first glance, it would be easy to make the assumption that he works in an office tower in the heart of the city.

The callus on his thumb and the tanned skin of his nose and cheeks tell a different story.

He works hard for a living, somewhere in the sun.

"Eden," I offer back as I slide my palm into his hand.

"As in the Garden of Eden? Are you the paradise I've been looking for?" he jokes. "Dance with me?"

It can't hurt. There's a certain comfort that comes from having the strong arms of a man wrapped around me as I move to the music.

It's heaven if the man can keep the same rhythm as me.

Dylan can. He always could.

The first time I asked Dylan to dance I was sixteen-years-old. He picked me up from a modern dance class so I could tutor him before football practice.

The ride in his shiny red Mustang was a treat, but the dance we shared before we left the rehearsal hall was what got my pulse racing and made my knees weak.

He took me in his muscular arms. I placed a hand on his broad shoulder and shivered when his hand slid down my back.

He twirled me in circles, his blue eyes never leaving mine, as the room cleared and my infatuation bloomed into a full-on crush.

It was a crush on the boy who saw me as the coach's daughter.

That's all I was to him until two nights ago.

"I hope you can keep up with me," I say to Hank.

He pulls me close, his breath skirting over my cheek. "I have no doubt that I can."

He leads, clumsily, as the music shifts from a throbbing fast beat to a slow, smooth pace.

He spins me once toward the bar. I steal a glance, not wanting to make eye contact with Dylan.

My heart stutters for a beat when I realize that the stool he was sitting on is vacant.

He's either left with someone or is on this dance floor, sweeping another woman off her feet, just as he did with me.

We had a moment in time that I never thought we would. It was a moment that I had dreamed of when I was a seven-teen-year-old girl watching the boy she wanted walk away from her.

"Eden?" Dylan's voice behind me drags my gaze over my shoulder.

I lock eyes with him.

He glances at Hank. "She's with me, pal."

"Are you?" Hank asks, disappointment edging his tone.

I look at his kind face. On another night, in another club, things might have been different.

"I requested our song next." Dylan moves to stand next to me. "You belong in my arms for that one."

Our song? My curiosity is strong enough to pull me away from my current dance partner.

I turn my attention back to him as couples dance past us. "It was nice meeting you, Hank."

I smile when he drags my hand to his mouth to plant a kiss on it. "It was my pleasure, Paradise."

When Hank turns to walk away, Dylan leans in until his lips brush against my ear. "He has no idea what paradise is. You taught me the meaning of the word two nights ago."

I close my eyes against the rush of desire I feel.

"Dance with me, Eden," he whispers, his hands gliding over my waist. "Let the music take you away."

I step closer to him just as the song changes again. The track we slow danced to the other night fills the air in a pounding beat.

It's fast, jumpy, and pulls the people around us apart as they flail their arms and bounce up and down.

Dylan tugs me against him and without any thought, we dance to our own rhythm, the same way we did when we were teenagers in the rehearsal hall.

CHAPTER FIFTEEN

DYLAN

I CAME to Veil East tonight with the hope that by some off chance, Eden would be here.

I found her wearing a red dress with her hair cascading down her back in waves. The same fiery color stained her lips. I wanted to kiss it off.

Yearned to kiss it off.

I watched from the shadows as she danced her way through two songs before I took a seat at the bar.

I was about to join her when a guy in a black suit approached her.

I studied every move between them. I saw her tug on the silver hoop in her right ear. I stared as he raked her from head-to-toe, his gaze stumbling on the fullness of her breasts under the fabric of her dress.

I swear to fuck he was as mesmerized with her as I was when I first saw her the other night. The truth is, I was captivated when I was seventeen and she asked me to dance when I went to pick her up for one of our tutoring sessions.

I'll never forget that night.

I fell in love with her as she looked up into my face with her big, blue eyes. I held her petite body in my arms and wished that I could take her in my car and drive her to a place where no one would ever find us.

"Are you thinking about how I'm going to wipe the floor with you in court?" Eden elbows me as we stand on the sidewalk outside the club.

People are milling about. Some want into the venue. Others escaped the crowded dance floor just as we did.

It was Eden's idea to take a breather outside.

I haven't broached the idea of going back to my place again. I'll let her set the pace tonight.

I shake my head. "No shop talk tonight."

"What do you want to talk about, Dylan?" She smiles.

Christ, she's so goddamn beautiful.

Her hair is wild. A light sheen of sweat dots her forehead and that red lipstick disappeared onto the rim of the glass of scotch I ordered after we danced.

I took the first sip. The rest slid between her lips when she tugged the glass from my hand.

She's already feeling the impact of that.

Her cheeks have flushed pink. Her breathing has slowed.

"Let's talk about high school."

I have no idea if this is the right time for us to stroll down memory lane, but there's only one way to find out.

"High school?" She spins in a circle. "I know that you couldn't let go of Barrett. No surprise there, but who else do you still see?"

"No surprise there?" I reach forward to brush a strand of

her hair away from the side of her face. "What the fuck does that mean?"

She laughs aloud, the sound clear and pure.

"You two were always like this." She crosses her middle finger over her index finger. "You're like peanut butter and jelly, or soup and sandwiches."

"You're hungry," I say with confidence, taking some pride in the fact that I still remember things about her that should have been easily forgotten. "You used to talk about food whenever you were hungry."

"Only for fries." She glances over her shoulder at a car stopping next to the curb. "I haven't had fries in forever and a day."

"I'll take you for fries, and we'll talk about high school."

"About Barrett?" She laughs. "He's hot so I get the appeal."

"He's not hot." Chuckling, I shake my head.

"Not as hot as you," she says quietly.

I'll gladly take the compliment. I'll also take the beautiful soft smile that came with it.

———

"SHOW OFF." She takes a bite of another fry. "Why am I not surprised that we're eating truffle fries and drinking champagne? I would have been happy with soggy fries from the fast food place across the street and a diet soda."

I would have been happy feeding her those soggy fries in my bed, but I'm trying to keep my aching dick out of this, for now.

Nova is co-owned and operated by a friend of mine.

Tyler Monroe is the head chef and the guy who can whip up a heaping plate of truffle fries on a moment's notice.

I sent him a text message on our way here.

We walked over since the restaurant is only a few blocks from the club, and Eden insisted that she needed the fresh air to sober up.

The champagne won't help with that, but I expect my explanation for why I ordered it will bring another smile to her face.

I lift my glass in the air. "Here's to my taking your client for every penny he has. I can already taste the sweetness of victory."

Her glass stays on the table even though the corners of her lips are tugging up into an almost grin. "I thought that you didn't want to talk about my pending win in the Alcester case. I've never lost in court, Dylan."

"How many cases have you tried? Two? Three?"

That parts her lips in a soft laugh. "Who else besides Barrett do you still see from school?"

"No one," I answer honestly. "I broke free of Chicago right out of the gate."

Her gaze drops. "New York City was calling your name?"

"NYU was." I reach for a fry. "That's not news to you."

"I remember." She watches as I chew. Her gaze slides to my neck when I swallow.

I like that she's interested enough to stare.

"Have you kept in touch with anyone, Eden?"

I don't give a shit if she still talks to Brittany, her best friend from senior year. I only want to know about Clark, the guy she was head over heels for. The fool who didn't know what he had in her.

"Do you remember Brittany?"

For fuck's sake.

I nod. "Sure. She was the cheese to your macaroni."

She tosses her head back in laughter. "She's the Barrett to my Colt."

I thought she'd forgotten the nickname everyone called me; everyone but her.

I was Dylan to her. Plain and simple. She didn't listen when I told her to call me Colt.

I secretly loved that she ignored my request and called me by my first name whenever she got the chance.

"Do you talk to anyone else?" I push, fishing for Clark's name and the confirmation that he's completely out of the picture.

"Like who?" She levels her gaze on me.

I spit it out because I want the subject swept under the rug tonight before I take her back to my bed. "Clark Dodson. What's the story with the two of you?"

The fry she just picked up falls to the table from her trembling hand. "There's no story to tell. Clark is part of my past."

CHAPTER SIXTEEN

DYLAN

IN COURT, this is the point when my pulse quickens and I go in for the proverbial kill.

I crave this look on the face of my clients' soon-to-be exes when they take the witness stand. It's an intoxicating mix of terror and fear.

Seeing it flash across Eden's expression only knots my gut.

I should feel a rush of relief knowing that Clark is history to her, but he's not.

If he were, she wouldn't have downed every drop of her champagne in one gulp.

She starts to reach for my glass, but I halt her hand with a brush of mine over it. "Eden."

Her eyes close briefly at the sound of my voice.

When they open she's found something again. It's composure or a sense of calm.

Whatever it is, it's a respite from the turmoil that crowded her just seconds ago.

She's pulled herself together in the blink of an eye. I'm an expert at it myself. I hate that she's had to perfect the skill too.

"I've had too much to drink." A soft faux laugh bubbles from somewhere shallow within her.

It's supposed to shift the focus from my question about Clark to her abrupt departure. I sense it coming. It's about to happen.

"I should go."

There it is.

"Where are you staying?" I'm not asking because I'm about to offer an invitation to my place. Curiosity is feeding my need to know where she's going to end up tonight.

"With Kurt's daughter." Her gaze falls to her watch. "Noelle. She has an extra bedroom. I'm sleeping there while I'm in the city."

I'll take her back to wherever the hell that is but first I want to know when she's planning on heading home to Buffalo.

Until now, I haven't given any thought to the fact that her time in New York is temporary. Our time together is fleeting.

"Kurt drafted you to be the star of his Manhattan dream team. What's the plan after the Alcester case?"

"You have it all wrong." She shakes her head. "Kurt treats every person who works for him as though they're the star of his dream team."

"Kurt Sufford does that?" I ask, sarcasm edging my tone. "You're serious?"

"What do you know about being the star of a dream team?" Her lips purse and I want nothing more than to reach across the table, tangle my fingers in her silky hair, and pull her in for a kiss.

She knows the dream, my dream, when I was eighteen and high on myself was to wear an NFL jersey.

Unfortunately, my skills weren't a match for my lofty ambition.

"I'm here until Mr. Alcester gets his due and his divorce," she says with a sweet smile. "After that, I'll go back to my open cases in Buffalo."

I start mentally drafting requests for continuances in my head. I don't like when a case drags, but this is an exception.

"We can settle this here and now, Dylan." Her voice drops to a more seductive tone. "The last offer Kurt presented to you is more than fair."

"That's a reach, and it's a no," I stress the last word. "You're in for a fight, Eden."

"I look forward to it."

I look forward to every day she's in Manhattan. I intend to take full advantage of our limited time together.

"Let's have dinner tomorrow night." I point at the plate of half-eaten fries. "I'll bring you back here for something more substantial than this."

"Why?" Her head tilts. "You don't want to talk more about high school do you? Because I don't think there's anything left to talk about. We've both changed since then and I, for one, prefer to focus on the present."

I'll close the door on high school if that's what she wants. Hell, I'll gladly bolt it shut so I never have to think about it again.

"Taking you out to dinner has nothing to do with the past," I say firmly so there's no question about my motivation. "This is about getting to know each other better now."

"Are you suggesting we go on a date?" She reaches for

the empty glass in front of her but stops herself before she makes a play for mine again.

"I am."

Her arms cross her chest. "We can't date each other."

I mimic her stance, crossing my arms over my chest. "Why not?"

"Pick a reason." Her hands fly into the air. "The Alcester case, our busy schedules, the fact that I'm leaving town in a few days."

"A few days?" I chuckle. "You were always an optimist. We're going to be tied up in court for weeks arguing every fine point."

"You'll settle when you see what I have up my sleeve."

I train my gaze on her brilliant blue eyes. "I won't settle. Dinner tomorrow, Eden."

"And then what?" Her finger circles in front of her. "We'll date until I leave for Buffalo? Why throw that complication into this?"

"The sex was that good."

Her tongue darts over her bottom lip in agreement. "The sex was a mistake."

I don't take it personally because she's lying through her perfectly straight white teeth. "We're adults. We can have fun while you're in New York."

I watch as she contemplates my words, her gaze skimming my face. "You're proposing that we have sex while I'm here? You want to do that while we're trying this case?"

"I'd prefer not to go down on you in open court, but I'm not opposed if that's what you're into."

A blush creeps over her cheeks. "I can't believe we're having this conversation."

"Believe it." I lean forward on the table. "You enjoyed the other night. You're open to more. Admit it, and we'll agree to spend time together outside the courtroom while you're in New York."

"It's not that simple, Dylan."

"It's that simple." I tap a finger over her hand. "I can keep my pleasure separate from my business. Can you?"

She drops her gaze to her lap before her eyes lock with mine. "I have before. I can do it again."

The admission shoots a spark of jealousy through me and a jolt of desire straight to my cock. I'm instantly hard.

She fucked a colleague.

Sweet, innocent Eden has changed in so many ways.

Damn, if that doesn't make me want her even more.

CHAPTER SEVENTEEN

EDEN

I THINK I just agreed to have sex with Dylan Colt again.

I shouldn't have, but he's right. The sex was that good.

"We need ground rules," I say. "I need those in place if this is going to work."

"Like what?"

I laugh aloud at his quick and expected response. Dylan was a rule-breaker in high school. He lived his life on his terms. Some of the time, it landed him in trouble. Most of the time, I envied his need not to conform.

"You have to divulge our relationship to your client."

"No." He huffs out a laugh. "There's no way in hell I'm telling Trudy that we're fucking each other."

"She has a right to know, Dylan."

"Our fucking," he pauses to circle his index finger in the air. "Our sleeping together will not impact my ability to represent her. The only thing Trudy cares about is the size of the settlement she'll be receiving and full custody of her daughters."

Arguing about how the case will end is useless at this point. Dylan's convinced his client is a saint. I know better, but Kurt taught me that biding time is one of the most effective weapons in a brilliant attorney's arsenal.

"Moving on," I skip past the urge to press him to tell Trudy.

I already told Troy that I share a history with Dylan. He assured me that he didn't care about any of that as long as I come to court prepared to do my job.

"Moving on," Dylan repeats with a roll of his hand in the air. "What's the next rule on your list?"

"This has to be casual." I sigh. "I'm going back to Buffalo soon."

"There's an expiry date on this." He nods. "I get that. I'm not following you back to Buffalo. My life is in Manhattan."

The sentiment mirrors mine from fifteen years ago.

Dylan was accepted to NYU. I was accepted to Juilliard. He was one of the first people I told.

It wasn't the only school that wanted me. My dad's face lit up when I showed him the acceptance letter from Ohio State. My grandpa earned his business degree there.

The decision wasn't an easy one.

On the night we graduated, Dylan assumed that I'd see him in New York three months later. He was about to leave for Europe to spend the summer exploring the countryside and the women across the pond.

I told him that I wouldn't be in New York in the fall. My future was in Ohio.

He turned and walked away from me, with only a simple goodbye.

I was seventeen. Romantic notions fueled my soul. I wanted him to tell me that he couldn't live in New York without me. I imagined him taking me into his arms and kissing me with the promise of what our nights in Manhattan would feel like.

None of that happened. He left. He never looked back.

I shouldn't have expected more. All I was to him was his coach's daughter and the girl who sometimes tutored him in math.

I was never the desire that lit a flame inside of him until a few nights ago at the club.

"I have a rule." He takes a sip of his champagne.

Envy draws my tongue over my bottom lip. I should have paced myself with my drink.

"What rule?" I ask with hesitation.

"Don't fuck anyone who works in Kurt's office."

He's blunt in a way I'm not used to. It sends a shiver racing down my spine. My core clenches in need.

"Have you met the people who work for Kurt?" I lift a brow.

He huffs out a laugh. "Several. I take it that you agree to my rule?"

"Anyone who works in Kurt's office is strictly off-limits." I cross my index fingers in an X. "Your rule doesn't include the rest of Manhattan, so I can get started on them tonight?"

His gaze drifts from my face to my neck. "You're mine until you go back to Buffalo."

"You don't strike me as the one woman type." I don't mean it as an insult. I expand on that so he'll understand the intention of my words. "You enjoy one-night stands. At least, I assume you do."

If he took offense, it's not there in the sexy smile he offers. "Variety is indeed the spice of my life, but you're only in town for a short time, and I want to focus all of my energy on you."

"Lucky me," I say with a bat of my eyelashes.

He leans forward, his eyes never leaving mine. "You have no idea, Eden."

The intensity of his gaze steals every rational thought from my mind.

There's no way that this is a good idea, but it'll be fun and that's been in short supply in my life.

"So we agree to the rules?" His gaze drops to the front of my low cut dress. "You're impossible to resist, Eden."

"We agree to the rules."

"I'm all yours until the case is over." He moves to stand. "I'll take you back to Noelle's place so you can sleep off the scotch and champagne. Tomorrow night at seven, we're having dinner. At nine, it's dessert in my bed."

CHAPTER EIGHTEEN

DYLAN

I WAS STOOD UP.

I'm a lawyer. I get that things pop up unexpectedly. In this case, Eden is chasing after something for the Alcester case.

I know that because she called my office and left a message with Gunner this afternoon. I was in the middle of a deposition. I told my assistant not to disturb me under any circumstances.

Gunner always takes me at my word.

Eden's message was short and to the point.

I can't make it tonight. I'm meeting with one of the skeletons from your client's closet.

I would have texted her a message back, but I don't have a cell number for her.

Calling Kurt's office to speak with her was a waste of time. Kurt's assistant shot me down with an excuse about Eden being tied up today.

The woman refused to hand over Eden's cell number.

Charm didn't work, so I pulled out my attorney card, but that was a fail.

I dropped the ball when I didn't ask Eden for her number last night.

She wouldn't let me take her back to Noelle's. She hopped into a taxi outside of Nova and disappeared around the corner.

"Sir, do you need me to do anything else today?"

My head pops up. "Jesus, Gunner. You scared the hell out of me. Clear your throat when you're coming down the corridor. Hum a tune. Anything, but this stealth shit you always pull on me."

I swear to fuck his lips curve up into a smirk before he loudly clears his throat.

"Too late for that." I rest my hands on my desk. "You can go."

He shakes his head. "I prefer to stay until you're done. Something may come up that I have to handle."

I don't know what the hell Gunner has going on during the few hours I give him to himself each day, but there has to be something he can do besides staring at me from the doorway of my office.

"Go home." I wave my hand in the air. "You've put in enough time for today."

"I can order something for dinner…for us."

I push back in my chair. "You're not a cheap date. The last time you ordered food in it was a five-course spread with an expensive bottle of red."

"Good taste isn't a liability, sir. It's an asset."

"It depends on whether you're the one stuck picking up the tab." I glance down at my watch. "I'll treat you to pizza."

"Pizza?" His nose scrunches. "I haven't had pizza in…"

"Too long," I interrupt as I slide to my feet. "A slice of

pizza, a beer, and then you go be you, Gunner. I need my space."

"I'll get ready," he quips. "Give me five minutes."

"Two minutes." I wave two fingers at him. "Be in the elevator in two minutes or my offer is off the table."

He darts out of my office and down the corridor, stomping his feet as he goes.

I didn't expect to be sitting across from him at a dinner table, but I plan on tracking Eden down as soon as my beer is empty.

I'm not ending my day without seeing her beautiful face.

———

THE BEST PIZZA in Manhattan is at a restaurant a block from my office.

It's over-priced, under-sauced, but the crust is exactly how I like it. It's crispy yet chewy. I've eaten enough bad pizza in my life to know that it's a feat to create the perfect crust.

When Gunner dove in for this third slice, I knew I was looking at a convert.

He'll be hitting the place up on the regular on his lunch break.

My assistant was prepared to extend our dinner into the evening. He suggested we take the party back to the office so he could run over the details for a case that I just took on.

Work can wait. I told Gunner as much when I directed him to the subway and told him to call it a night.

I took off in the opposite direction.

I'm still on a quest to find Eden. That's why I'm standing on the sidewalk outside the building that's home to the offices of Sufford, Lake & Chisholm.

It's mid-evening, which means that anyone with a life outside of work has left for the day.

I'm banking on the fact that Eden hasn't lost her drive to commit to whatever is in front of her.

That's what took her to the rehearsal hall virtually every night during senior year.

I stalk into the lobby of the building, heading straight for the night guard who mans the desk near the elevators.

"Can I help you…" His voice trails. "Dylan? Is that you?"

It pays to help people who need it.

Myron, the guard, sat next to me on the subway one day when I was heading back to the office after court.

He was despondent and broke. I was feeling uncharacteristically generous after winning a case.

In the six hours before we met, Myron was let go from his job as a member of the cleaning crew at one of the city's museums.

He was cut in the middle of his shift. He went home to the house he shared in Queens with his wife of twenty-two years to plan out how he'd break the bad news to her once she was done work for the day.

She wasn't behind a desk in her office on Wall Street. She was on the dick of her boss in the bed she shared every night with Myron.

Myron told me his story as we took the train uptown.

I took on his case, we shook on the promise of a percentage of his settlement, and I got to work on drafting the papers that afternoon.

I topped it off with a new job for him. He worked security at the building that houses my office until he was reassigned to work here.

He's got money in the bank, a pension to look forward to, and a new girlfriend who only has eyes for him.

"Myron." I pat him on the shoulder. "I'm looking for Eden Conrad. She's filling in for Kurt Sufford temporarily."

"The beauty from Buffalo?" He smiles. "She slips me a candy bar almost every night on her way out."

That doesn't surprise me.

The smile on Myron's face doesn't surprise me either. He's always friendly as fuck and eager to help.

Her cell number is at his disposable. I'll be calling her before I exit this building.

"She's here."

That's more than I could have hoped for. "Eden is here?"

"That she is." He nods. "She just went back up with some take-out. It looks like she'll be stuck here for most of the night."

Not if I have a say in it.

I glance at the elevators. "I'm going to run up and surprise her."

His brow knits. "She's up there alone. I should probably call to let her know you're here."

"We're old high school friends." I toss him a wink. "Give me the chance to surprise her like old times."

The only time I ever surprised Eden was when I showed up to her dance recital. I'll never forget the look on her face or the tears in her eyes.

"How can I say no to that?" He starts toward the elevator. "You need a keycard to get up at this time of day. I'll swipe mine and send you on your way."

CHAPTER NINETEEN

EDEN

THIS IS the very reason why some adults need to wear bibs.

I stare down at the large red splotch on the front of my white blouse.

Everyone in the office has been raving about the spaghetti at Calvetti's so I put in an order for take-out.

I admit it's the best pasta I've ever had, but I dropped a forkful of sauce onto my blouse.

Dammit.

I glance around my empty office to the darkness in the corridor beyond it.

I'm the only one here.

There's no harm in running the blouse down to the dry cleaners two blocks over.

They're open until nine.

The only problem is that I have nothing to put on to replace my shirt. I can't race around Manhattan in a lace bra.

I suppose I could, but I'd rather not get arrested for indecent exposure. One plus is that I would save big on attorney fees since I'd represent myself.

I giggle as I think about my defense.

"Your honor, I blame it all on the tomato sauce," I say as I unbutton my blouse. "I had to make a choice. Save the shirt, or save face. I chose the shirt because it fits perfectly."

I hold open the front of the blouse. "I present Exhibit A. My breasts. They look amazing in this blouse."

"They look better out of it."

I spin on my heel at the sound of the familiar male voice coming from the doorway of my office.

A smile slides over Dylan Colt's lips. "What the fuck is going on here, and how do I get in on this action?"

———

I WRAP the sauce-stained blouse around me. "What the hell are you doing?"

"I just asked you that same question." He glances past me to the view of Manhattan through the window of my office.

It's dark, so all that awaits the eye is a sprinkling of lights from the buildings across the street.

"You realize people can see in here, right?"

My gaze darts over my shoulder to the window. "I'm not naked, Dylan."

"Close." He exhales on a sigh. "Take off the blouse. You can wear my jacket."

The jacket is off his shoulders before I can protest.

He shoves it at me, but I don't take it.

"Why are you here?" I repeat my question. "How did you get up here?"

"Myron is an old friend." He takes a measured step closer

to me. "I told him you were another old friend of mine, so he let me up."

"I'll never buy him another candy bar," I mutter.

"Sure you will," Dylan responds with a smirk. "Take the jacket, Eden. We can wash the blouse at my place."

The way he so effortlessly mentions going back to his place both irritates and excites me. He's so sure of himself.

I can't blame him for that.

The man is built for sex. Everything about him screams that he's incredible in bed.

He is.

My experience with him was limited, but it was still the best sexual encounter I've ever had.

I shake my head to chase away thoughts of his naked body.

Jesus, he's breathtaking in and out of a suit.

"You're thinking about fucking me."

I spit out a laugh that sounds more like a shriek. "What? No. Why would you even say that?"

"Your nipples." He circles a finger in the air, pointing at my hardened nipples under the lace of my bra. "Your nipples are thinking about fucking me."

I cross my arms over my chest. "It's cold in here."

"It's not." He tosses the jacket onto one of the chairs in front of my desk. "Do you want my shirt? You can wear it back to my place. I'm good with just the jacket."

His cufflinks are off and in the pocket of his pants.

What is wrong with him?

"No." I shake my head. "I have to work. You need to leave."

"You're coming with me." He slides off his tie. "Come home with me. I'll wash and dry your blouse. My laundry skills are impressive."

"That's not a good idea."

"It's a fantastic idea." His hands start on the buttons of his shirt. "We can share a bottle of wine. You'll have an orgasm or three."

"Three?" I laugh. "You're way too cocky."

The shirt slips off of him. "Too cocky? Is that a thing?"

My eyes dart over his muscular chest and his abs. "Is what a thing?"

He huffs out a laugh. "Put on my shirt."

I toss my stained blouse onto my desk before I take his dress shirt in my hand. "I'm leaving as soon as my blouse is cleaned and dried."

"That works."

Staring at him, I button his shirt up. "Why did you come here tonight?"

"I came for a kiss."

My heart flutters in my chest at his admission. "You came here just to kiss me?"

He answers me with a soft brush of his lips over mine. "I'd go anywhere just to kiss you."

Our kiss intensifies when his hand finds my waist. He pulls me closer to him, pressing his body to mine.

I feel how erect he is. I hear his need in the moan that escapes him when I tug his bottom lip between my teeth.

"It's time to go," he breathes the words into my mouth. "Now, Eden."

I don't protest. I don't want to. All I do want is to be back in his bed.

CHAPTER TWENTY

Eden

IF SOMEONE HAD TOLD me a month ago that I'd be standing in Dylan Colt's apartment on Fifth Avenue wearing nothing but one of his dress shirts and my lingerie, I would have laughed in their face.

I thought Dylan was part of my past.

I admit that I held out hope that our paths would cross again at some point, but I gave up that fairytale dream ten years ago.

"Your blouse and skirt are in the trusty hands of my dry cleaner." Dylan walks into his bedroom. He's still wearing his suit jacket, his trousers, and a smile.

He garnered a few second glances on the walk from my office to here.

You can't blame anyone for staring at him. He looks like a Greek God in that suit without a shirt on.

"When will I get them back?" I tug on the bottom of his dress shirt.

He noticed a few drops of sauce on the front of my light blue skirt while we were riding the elevator up to his place.

Before we reached his floor, he had his dry cleaner on the phone.

He ordered me to drop the skirt once we were inside his apartment. After that, he took off out the door again with my sauce-stained clothes in his hand.

"Tomorrow morning." He rakes me with a heated glance. "You want to fuck me."

Crossing my arms over my chest, I roll my eyes. "What is it with you? Do you use that line on all the women you sleep with?"

They're my words, but they sting.

I know this arrangement is temporary. Once I'm back in Buffalo, Dylan will be a fond memory of my past again.

This time that memory will include phenomenal sex, but it will still just be a memory.

He'll go back to his life in this tower in the sky he lives in.

I'll go back to my two-bedroom condo in downtown Buffalo.

"I'm stating the obvious." He shrugs out of his jacket, hanging it on the back of a chair that faces the window. "Let's not bring up the other women I've been with."

I'm fine with that.

Dylan's number in high school was higher than my number to date.

He never outright told me that he slept with seven different girls in senior year. I heard about it from my friends, or in one case, one of the girls he took to bed blurted it out during a study session.

I stopped her from sharing any details by reminding her

that she had an exam the following day that she couldn't afford to fail.

I bounce back to the subject of my clothes because I have no intention of spending the night.

"Why didn't you just throw my shirt and my skirt in your washing machine?"

His hands fall to the leather belt at his waist. "That sauce is going to be a bitch to get out. I have talent, but it only reaches so far."

"You'll just have to spend the night."

Pointing at his hands, I shake my head slightly. "I'll wear this shirt home. That belt around my waist will make it look like a dress."

"This belt?" He slides it from his pants in one smooth motion. "What if I tell you that you can't borrow the shirt or the belt? You won't parade around the streets of Manhattan in a bra and a pair of panties."

Maybe it's the attorney in me, but I take the statement as a challenge. I unbutton his shirt and slide it off, revealing the white lace bra and matching panties underneath. "I'll do it."

His gaze is riveted to my body. "You wouldn't. Not you."

I reach behind me to unclasp the bar, sliding the straps down my arms until it falls to the floor at my feet. My hands drop to my hips. "You don't know me anymore, Dylan. You'd be surprised at some of the things I've done."

He steps out of his pants. "What have you done?"

"Let's not talk about the men I've had sex with," I whisper. "You don't want to hear about them, do you?"

His right hand disappears inside his boxer briefs. I watch as he grips his erection under the fabric.

Envy shoots through my veins. I want to touch it, kiss it, and lick it until he shudders from pleasure brought by my hands and mouth.

"How many?" he asks with a deep rasp in his voice.

"Men have I fucked?" I ask back, my hands sliding over my stomach to the waistband of my panties.

"How many men, Eden?" His gaze is transfixed. He can't tear his eyes away from the path of my fingers as they dive under the lace.

I moan loudly when my hand parts my folds.

"Jesus," he hisses loudly. "How many men have fucked that sweet cunt?"

I close my eyes against the rush of raw need I feel. I circle my clit, bringing myself closer and closer to the edge.

"Eden." My name lashes off his tongue.

I open my eyes slowly. His boxer briefs are pushed down to mid-thigh. His fist circles his thick cock.

It's the most erotic thing I've ever seen.

He pumps his cock once, and then again, drawing a bead of pre-cum to the tip.

"Tell me," he spits out between clenched teeth.

I step forward, my fingertip still drawing a tight circle over my clit. Soft moans escape my lips, brought to the surface by my need to come, and the sight of Dylan's big hand sliding over his cock.

"Have you ever thought about me while you're doing that?" I whisper.

He nods, his free hand reaching to curl around my wrist. He yanks my hand from my panties, dragging it up to his lips.

He pushes just the tips of my fingers into his mouth. His tongue brushes over them. "Christ, Eden. You're so sweet."

I stare at the look on his face, wanting to imprint it on my brain forever.

It's there because of me.

He wants me. He needs me.

I tug my hand from his, slide down to my knees, and reward myself with a sweep of my tongue over the head of his cock.

I finally get my first taste of Dylan Colt's desire.

CHAPTER TWENTY-ONE

DYLAN

GODDAMMIT.

I tangle both of my hands in Eden's hair, twisting it at the roots.

That lures a breathy moan from her that vibrates along the length of my dick.

She can't swallow it all, but I don't give a fuck.

This is too good. It's so damn good that I can't help but let out a stuttered groan when I feel the tip of her tongue lash against the underside of my crown.

"Like that," I manage to form two words before another heady growl pours out of me.

I thrust into her mouth, riding the pleasure as she grips the root of my dick and pumps in perfect rhythm with the motion of her tongue.

She licks and sucks like I'm the best thing she's ever tasted.

I pray that I am.

Jesus, I wish I were the only man she's ever had.

I up the pace. Pure need drives my hips forward with each plunge of my cock between her lips.

I fuck her mouth, listening to the sweet sounds she makes.

I could come like this.

I tug on her hair. "My turn."

She shakes her head, upping the pace of her strokes.

"Stop." I pull harder, drawing a wince from her. "Get on the bed."

Her hands glide up my body as she pulls herself to her feet.

I kiss her hard with my hands cupping her cheeks. "On the bed."

She steps backward, her eyes glued to mine. "I wasn't done. I want more."

"You'll get more." I eye her underwear. "Take those off, or I'll fucking destroy them."

Her gaze falls to the front of her panties. "You want me that much?"

I reach for her arms, pushing her onto the bed.

She falls onto her back, her tits bouncing, her hair whipping around her face.

I bracket my hands on either side of her shoulders. Staring down at her, I say what my body has been screaming since I was eighteen-years-old. "I want you more than I've ever wanted anyone."

Lifting her head from the bed, her lips purse. I give her the kiss she so desperately wants, before I lower myself down her body and take what I want.

———

I'VE NEVER BEEN a man prone to addiction, but her taste unravels me.

I lick and suck on her beautiful cunt, luring sounds from her that shoot straight to my aching cock.

I've never come from the taste of a woman, but this is different.

I'm pulsing in need.

I feel another drop of pre-cum when my dick brushes against my inner thigh.

I tongue her deeper, pushing her thighs apart as my fingers sweep over the swollen nub of her clit.

Everything about her is perfect. She's made for me.

"Dylan." My name comes out in a whisper. "I'm going to…"

"I know," I growl before I lash my tongue against her clit.

She crashes over the edge in a pulsating orgasm.

I slide two fingers into her pussy so I can feel her come. It's so tight, so smooth, and so fucking good.

I suck in a deep breath, willing myself to control the desperation I feel until I'm inside of her.

I move slowly, trailing kisses over her soft skin as I make my way up her body.

I stop when I reach her breasts, circling each of her hardened nipples with my tongue. "Your nipples are sensitive, aren't they?"

She glances down at me. A sated look floats over her expression. "So sensitive."

I bite the right one before I give the same attention to the left.

She whines through it all. "Dylan, stop."

"You don't want me to stop," I say before I plant a soft kiss on her lips. "You want me to fuck you."

Her eyes scan my face. "You're really handsome."

A smile tugs on the corners of my mouth. "You're gorgeous, Eden."

"Did you think that back…"

I halt her words with a deep kiss. When I pull back, I stare into her piercing blue eyes. "I've always thought you were the most beautiful woman on this earth."

Her bottom lip trembles. "I want you."

I want to hold her, protect her, and shield her from everything wrong in this world.

Her gaze darts to the box of condoms on my nightstand. "Now, Dylan."

I steal one last look at her face before I move to stand.

Sheathing my cock with a shaking hand, I draw in enough air to fill my lungs even though I still feel like I can't catch my breath.

I crawl over her slowly, savoring the anticipation, soaking in her beauty.

Once I'm on top, I glide the tip of my dick over her core. "You're slick. So wet."

Her tongue darts out over her bottom lip. "Kiss me."

I do. I press my mouth to hers just as I slide my cock into her tight cunt.

I fuck her slowly and gently until she begs for more. Then I flip her over and take her the way she wants with long, powerful thrusts.

CHAPTER TWENTY-TWO

DYLAN

"MR. COLT? SIR?"

There's no way in hell that this is happening again.

My hand runs over the sheet beside me. I come up empty.

"Dammit," I mutter. "Where's Eden?"

"Eden?" Gunner's voice ticks up an octave. "Are you talking about Eden Conrad?"

I force one of my eyes open. Sunlight is pouring in the room. My assistant is dressed in his usual garb even though today is Saturday.

Wait a goddamn minute. It's Saturday.

"Why are you here?" I wave a hand in his general direction. "Shouldn't you be at home annoying the hell out of someone else?"

"Is Eden Conrad your girlfriend?" he presses on. "She's representing Mr. Alcester. She called the office to leave a message. I never forget a name, especially one as nice as Eden."

I manage to open both eyes. "Go home."

"We had plans this morning, sir." His tone edges on frustration. "It's important."

It can't be as important as Eden.

I ate her to another orgasm last night after we fucked. I couldn't resist.

She fell asleep in my arms afterward. I thought it was a guarantee that she'd be here this morning since her clothes are still at the dry cleaners.

I had visions of breakfast in bed, sex in the shower, and then I'd run to grab her shirt and skirt sometime this afternoon.

I scrub my hand over my face. "What plans?"

"Brunch with Mrs. Jenkinson." He scribbles his hand in the air. "She's ready to sign on the dotted line with a retainer check in hand."

I remember now.

I did set that up. I'll do business every day of the week, any hour of the day.

Boundaries don't fit into my business model. Extra hourly fees for weekend meetings do.

"I don't need you to hold my hand through this." I shoot Gunner a look. "I can handle it."

"She requested that I be there."

I swear to God he blushes at that admission.

Martha Jenkinson is more than double his age, but if she floats his boat and they play safe, who am I to judge?

"I'll handle the paperwork. You'll take over after that." I swing my legs over the side of the bed, taking care to keep my dick covered. "I'll meet you downstairs in twenty minutes."

His gaze drops to his watch. "Eighteen would be optimum. Mrs. Jenkinson requested brunch at Axel Tribeca at eleven. It's the restaurant inside the Bishop Hotel."

Eleven?

I point at his watch. "What the hell time is it?"

"Ten-fifteen on the dot," he says proudly. "We'll make it with time to spare."

I shake my head. "I can't remember the last time I slept this late."

"It does a body good." Gunner offers words of wisdom that I'm guessing he lifted from a billboard in Times Square or an ad he saw online. "It's nice to see you enjoying life outside the office."

I'd enjoy it more if I knew when Eden left and why she took off without her clothes.

———

EXITING AXEL TRIBECA, I pull my phone out of the pocket of my suit jacket.

I silenced it before the meeting with Martha Jenkinson.

My clients pay me enough to guarantee they have my undivided attention when I'm sitting in front of them or chatting with them on the phone.

Gunner is the go-to if a problem crops up during my one-on-one client time. His gaze drifted to the screen of his phone only once during brunch. He didn't make eye contact with me after he read the text message that popped up, so it wasn't vital.

I scroll through the log of missed calls and text messages.

There's nothing from Eden.

It's closing in on one p.m. now. I can swing by the dry cleaners, pick up her pressed skirt and shirt, and put them back in her hands.

I type out a quick text to her.

Dylan: Thanks for taking the time to say goodbye this morning.

Her reply is quick.

Eden: Do I detect a hint of sarcasm? Does someone feel used?

The sad face emoji she tacks onto the end of the message draws a laugh from me.

I catch the eye of a woman standing a couple of feet away from me.

Normally, convenience like this wouldn't go unappreciated by me. I'd strike up a conversation and suggest we go into the restaurant for a drink. By mid-afternoon, we'd be back at my place.

She tosses her light brown hair over her shoulder with a wave of her fingers.

I respond with a brisk nod and a drop of my eyes to my phone's screen.

Dylan: You can use me whenever the hell you want. Now is good.

Eden: I'm working on destroying your client's reputation, but I'm available tonight.

The scent of cloying sweet perfume catches my attention.

I turn my head to find the woman I noticed moments ago, standing next to me.

"I'm Kim." She extends a hand with bright red fingernails.

I ignore it. "I'm leaving."

Her mouth pouts into a scowl. "My loss."

I leave it at that, brushing past her to make my way down the crowded sidewalk.

Before I can respond to Eden's text, she's sent another.

Eden: Did you get my clothes back from the drycleaners?

The drycleaners is my next stop before I put in a few hours at the office.

Dylan: Your blouse and skirt will be waiting for you at my place tonight. Does 8 work for you?

Eden: Eight works. What do I owe you for the dry cleaning?

I stop to wait for a crossing light.

Dylan: A picture of you in whatever the hell you ran out of my place wearing.

By the time the light changes she still hasn't replied.

She didn't take the dress shirt she had on last night, and my belt was still where I left it on the floor of my bedroom.

My phone chimes when I turn the corner toward the subway station.

I drop my gaze to the screen and the picture attached to the simple message she sent.

Eden: I found this in your closet.

"Jesus." I breathe out on a heavy sigh. I wasn't expecting this.

It's obvious that she's sitting on a bed.

Her beautiful legs are in view. The picture only captures the bottom half of the jersey she's wearing. The hem hits her mid-thigh.

I wore that football jersey in every game I played in high school.

My dad brought it to New York in a clear garment bag right after I bought my apartment. I told him to take it back home, but he insisted on hanging it in my walk-in closet. He told me I'd thank him one day when I had a son who wanted to pick up the game.

It all went back to the fact that I wore his high school football jersey when I was a twelve-year-old kid tossing the ball with him on Sunday afternoons.

I haven't looked at my old jersey in years. It didn't mean anything to me until now.

Another message pops up on my screen.

Eden: You'll have to earn it back, Colt.

I'm instantly hard. I don't want the damn thing back. I want her to wear it, sleep in it, keep it.

I type back a simple response.

Dylan: We'll talk terms tonight.

Eden: I can't wait.

CHAPTER TWENTY-THREE

EDEN

BUTTERFLIES FLIT in my stomach as I approach Dylan's building.

I've been thinking about him all day. It's impossible not to.

We had another incredible night last night.

After we made love, we both fell asleep. I woke to the sound of my phone ringing.

Dylan didn't budge so I unraveled myself from his arms and sought out my purse.

The call was from Noelle. She was worried that I wasn't home, and since she hadn't been able to reach me for hours, she stopped sending unanswered text messages and called me instead.

I could hear the anxiety in her voice. I knew it wasn't all about me being MIA, so I took to Dylan's closet to find something to wear home.

I couldn't believe my eyes when I spotted his old high school football jersey.

I slid it on over my bra and panties and left his apartment.

The look on Noelle's face when I finally got home was one for the record books.

She didn't ask anything after getting a glimpse of the name stitched on the back of the jersey.

COLT.

We spent the next two hours talking about her dad, her work, and a cute guy she met on the subway.

We finally called it a night at three a.m., but not before promising each other that we'd have dinner together this coming week.

I slow as I get closer to Dylan's building when I spot his familiar frame standing outside the doors with his back to me.

The man can work a pair of jeans and a black sweater just as well as a tailored suit.

I'm glad I opted for casual tonight too. I'm wearing faded, ripped jeans and a black blouse. I don't want a repeat of last night's saucy mess, so I choose a dark color to camouflage any potential food clumsiness on my part.

"Dylan," I call out his name.

He turns instantly, a bright smile taking over his gorgeous mouth.

His phone is to his ear. I watch as he says something I can't quite make out before he tucks the phone in the front pocket of his jeans.

He rakes me over. "Great minds think alike."

I laugh. "You can't go wrong with jeans and a black blouse for a date."

The last word floats off my lips so effortlessly.

We're going on a date. I'm on a date with Dylan Colt.

"Or a black sweater." He pinches the front of his V-neck sweater. "Are you hungry?"

"Famished," I confess, rubbing my stomach. "I haven't eaten all day."

I wait for the expected comment about him not eating pussy all day. It was one of his tried and true lines when he was eighteen.

My reaction would always be the same. I'd grimace and shoo him away with a swat of my hand on his shoulder. Secretly, I longed to feel his mouth on me. I envied every girl who had been with him.

"I made a reservation." He gestures down the sidewalk. "It's just a block over."

I don't bother asking what we'll be eating, because I don't care.

The details don't matter.

What matters is the way he's looking down at me. It's the same way he looked at me when I was seventeen, and he was the boy I wanted more than anything in the world.

———

"PANCAKES FOR DINNER might be the best thing ever." I laugh as we exit what can only be described as an elegant breakfast retreat.

It's a tiny place just off Park Avenue that serves decadent breakfast staples to a discerning dinner crowd.

There's no jacket or tie requirement and you won't find an imported bottle of beer there.

We sipped on mimosas and ate the most delicious pancakes slathered in berries and a bourbon maple syrup glaze.

Candied bacon was the side.

I'm stuffed and happier than I've been in a long time.

"It's one of my favorite places in the city." Dylan turns to face me. "I've never brought anyone here before."

Something sparks inside of me.

Joy or relief, maybe it's the satisfaction of knowing that he chose to share a special place with me.

"They need to open a location in Buffalo." I laugh. "I'd never have to cook for myself again."

His brow furrows. "Do you live alone?"

I nod. "It's just me. No cats or dogs. No birds. Absolutely no roommates."

He chuckles. "Your dad used to say that he expected you to take care of him when he retired. I always pictured him living under the same roof as you once he gave up coaching. Did he settle in Buffalo too?"

It's been years, but some grief can't be measured in time. It burrows into a spot inside of you and never leaves. That's how it was for me. How it still is.

"My dad died," I manage to say in a soft voice. "He's gone."

Dylan's hand darts to his mouth. His eyes widen in shocked disbelief. "What? When?"

"Three years ago." I look up at the lights of the city trying to find my center.

I still cry but only on days that remind me of him. His birthday, my birthday, the day my mom died when I was ten-years-old.

He never fully recovered from her death. At times, he'd wish that cancer would claim him too. It did.

"How?" Dylan's head is shaking back and forth in denial.

Every player on my dad's team had a place in his heart. Dylan was included in that. They may not have always seen eye-to-eye, but my dad would have done anything for

Dylan. He saw potential in him and all the boys on the team.

"Cancer," I give the short answer because the details of the treatments, the suffering, and the last agonizing months aren't important to anyone but me.

I was an only child.

"Eden." His hands leap to my face. He cradles it in his palms as he gazes into my eyes. "I'm so sorry."

I swallow back the urge to cry. I see the same pain in his eyes that I felt when the doctor told me that my dad was gone. I was holding his hand. I heard the unmistakable sound of the monitor when his heart stopped, but still, I hoped.

I prayed for a miracle that never came.

"I wish I would have known," he says on a heavy exhale. "Fuck. I should have known about this."

"You know now," I offer quietly. "He always told me to remember the good times. He'd want you to do the same thing."

His gaze drops to the sidewalk. "He was an incredible man. One of the best."

He was. He was my hero. He'll always be.

CHAPTER TWENTY-FOUR

DYLAN

COACH CONRAD IS GONE.

The earth kept spinning after he checked out. How the hell is that possible?

The man was a force of nature, unlike any I've known before or since.

He was committed to raising his daughter with caring guidance and a trusting heart. He loved Eden more than anything, but he gave her room to find out who she was and where she fit in the world.

He did the same for me.

He never held back an opinion regardless of how much it bit into the self-esteem of the person it was directed at.

He was compassionate in his delivery of criticism, but he expected the best from everyone in his path.

Coach made me a better man.

"What do you want to do now?" Eden tugs at the front of my sweater.

I know she's trying to ease me back to reality. The news of her dad's death is hitting me hard.

I feel the loss of someone who once mattered greatly to me, but more than that, I feel for her.

Her dad was her rock. He kept her anchored to her dreams and her future.

"What do you want to do?" I tilt her head up with a finger to her chin.

"Dance," she says in a whispered tone. "I want to dance."

I tug her into my arms. "Here?"

She looks around at the people passing us by on the sidewalk. It's Saturday night in New York City. The streets are filled with folks out looking for a good time.

"Here?" she parrots back with a giggle. "There's no music."

I start to sway us back and forth. "Since when do you need music to dance?"

Her arms curl around my neck. "Good point."

I twirl her in a circle, luring a breathy moan from her lips.

"I know a place we can dance," I offer. "I think you'll like it."

"Is it your apartment?" Her eyes narrow. "Does it involve taking off our clothes?"

"There's an idea I can get behind." My hand glides down to tap the top of her ass. "Or a behind I want to get behind."

"Dylan." My name slips from her lips in a purr. "There is plenty of time for that later."

"We have all night." I slide my lips over hers, savoring the sweet taste of her. "Tonight, you won't run and hide when I fall asleep."

"I'm not making any promises."

I lean in again, brushing my lips over her ear. "I'll tie you to the bed if I have to."

Her breath stutters for a second before she moves back to look into my eyes. "Take me dancing first."

I'll give her anything she wants. "Follow me."

Her hand slips into mine, and we start down the street toward an experience I know she'll never forget.

———

WE EXIT the Uber just off Columbus Avenue on the Upper West Side.

Eden's gaze volleys from left to right. I know that she's trying to figure out where the hell I'm taking her.

"This way," I say, reaching for her hand.

I guide her down the street of businesses shuttered for the night. A few remain open luring patrons in with signs promising the best cup of coffee in the city, or cocktails for half price.

Once we reach our destination, I turn to face her.

Questions are dancing in her eyes. She trusts me. At least, I hope to fuck she does.

"I had a feeling you'd want to dance tonight, so I made some arrangements." I lean down to kiss her cheek. "We'll dance as many dances as you want. We can stay as late as you like, but once we leave, we're going back to my place."

Her gaze jumps to the non-descript dark green door behind me. It's tucked between a shoe store and a flower shop. Both have closed signs hanging in their windows.

The green door leads down a flight of stairs to a spot that I discovered a year ago when I was asked by the owner to meet him here to talk about his crumbling marriage.

A month later, he opted for counseling instead of divorce. I didn't charge him a dime for the three consultations we had.

In exchange, he gave me his word that he'd return the favor whenever I needed it.

I needed it tonight, so I gave him a call earlier.

"Agreed." Eden sighs. "Where exactly are we going?"

I rap on the door three times with my fist before I lock eyes with her. "You're about to find out."

CHAPTER TWENTY-FIVE

Eden

CHARMING DOESN'T BEGIN to describe this place.

Our flight down a steep staircase brought us to an intimate club. No more than two-dozen people could fit in here at any time, but tonight it's almost empty.

There's a bartender in a flowered patterned vest and matching bowtie behind a sleek glass bar. Her red hair is tugged up into a tight ponytail. Her eye makeup is dramatic.

On a stage that lines the wall opposite the bar are four men. All are dressed alike in black vests and bowties. White dress shirts and black pants complete their muted look.

The quartet is playing a soft jazz tune. The dance floor directly in front of them is vacant. Every small circular wooden table is empty except for one. There's a man with salt and pepper hair sitting next to it in a chair. An amber colored liquid fills half a glass tumbler on the table in front of him.

I glance back to see if the man who opened the green door

is behind us, but he's not. He must not have followed us down the stairs after he locked the door once we entered.

"Billy," Dylan calls out. "I didn't think you'd hang around."

The man at the table turns and smiles. It's so wide and genuine that it's disarming. Crow's feet pinch at the corners of his brown eyes.

"Dylan Colt," he says, rising to his feet. "You made it."

"Was there any doubt I would?" Dylan reaches for Billy's hand as he approaches us.

Billy takes it for a quick shake before his palm is pointed in my direction. "You must be Eden. You're more beautiful than Dylan described."

I shake his hand, smiling at him. "It's nice to meet you."

"You're a dancer." His tone is soft. "I hope you find our dance floor acceptable."

I glance past him to the parquet wood floor. Every inch of this club is exquisite. It's obvious from the detailed wood-work on the archways that it was built more than a lifetime ago.

"I think it will be perfect," I say sincerely. "I can't wait to take a spin."

Billy's gaze centers on me. "I won't keep you. Drink as much as you like. Dance until your legs give out. Everything is on the house."

Dylan raises his hand in protest. "No, Billy. I'll cover the cost of your staff. You closed down the place tonight just for us. I know that's costing you a pretty penny."

He brushes Dylan's comments off with a shake of his head. "You saved my marriage. That's priceless. Consider this my thank you gift to you."

Just as I look up at Dylan, he looks down at me. "I'm not always the bad guy. Sometimes a marriage is worth saving."

He read my mind or my expression. He knew that I would wonder what Billy was talking about.

"Mine was worth saving." Billy wiggles his ring finger at me. The lights above us catch the diamonds in the thick gold band that circles his finger. "Our twenty-eighth anniversary is next month."

"Congratulations," I offer with a smile. "That's amazing."

"It's a gift." Billy glances over his shoulder at the stage. "I'm cutting into your time together. I'm going home to the Mrs. You two enjoy your night."

"We will," Dylan says quickly. "Thanks again, Billy."

"No thanks are necessary. It's the least I can do." He reaches for the glass from the table, raising it in the air. "Here's to the next great love story. I think I may be playing a small part in it as we speak."

———

NEITHER OF US reacted to Billy's comment about his part in the next great love story even though we knew he was talking about the two of us.

Dylan walked Billy to the staircase and then ordered us each a glass of white wine from the bartender.

We're on the dance floor now enjoying a slow song with a soothing melody.

I trail my fingers over the back of Dylan's neck, loving the feeling of his hands on my waist.

I look up into his light blue eyes. They haven't changed at all since the first time I ever saw them. If anything, they've become more vibrant and intense.

"What are you thinking?" Dylan asks quietly.

We move slowly in sync, keeping in perfect rhythm to the song. "That you saved someone's marriage."

A grin ghosts his mouth. "That shocks you."

I tilt my head to take in the expression on his face. It's hard to read. "It does shock me a little."

"Why?" He smirks.

"I'm a divorce attorney too." I let him lead me closer to the band. "At the end of the day, broken marriages pay our bills."

"They weigh on us too." He spins me around.

He's right. I've had people come into my office in Buffalo after an argument with their spouse about something as insignificant as a wet towel left on the bathroom floor. I always give those potential clients the same advice. I tell them to go home and take some time to sort out what they're feeling.

When I reach out a couple of weeks later, most have no need for my services anymore because they've kissed and made up with their partner.

In those cases, I didn't save a marriage. I avoided a lot of paperwork that I'd never end up filing because the client would have called off the proceedings a day or two after the initial argument with their spouse.

"How did you end you being an attorney?" Dylan slows his pace.

I don't want to talk about how my goal to be a professional dancer on Broadway fell victim to the car crash. Once I realized that I'd never take to a stage on the Great White Way, I fell back to the dream my mom gave up when she found out she was pregnant with me.

"My mom always wanted to be a lawyer."

I smile when I think about her light brown hair and blue eyes. She was breathtakingly beautiful even when cancer caught her in its clutches.

She shaved her head the day before my tenth birthday, so I did the same.

I got in trouble for it, but that lasted less than a minute. My sacrifice meant everything to her.

She gave up law school and a career to spend her days raising me. Becoming an attorney was the greatest gift I could give to her.

"She'd be proud of you." Dylan brushes his lips over my forehead. "Coach would be too."

I rest my head on his chest as we dance through the end of the song and into the beginning of the next.

I haven't had a night like this in a very long time. I never want it to end.

CHAPTER TWENTY-SIX

DYLAN

GUILT GNAWS at me as I unlock the door to my apartment.

Somewhere in the recesses of my mind, I held firm to the notion that at some point, in this lifetime, I'd be able to apologize to Coach Conrad face-to-face and man-to-man.

When he didn't return my calls after the accident, it felt like I'd been banished to my own personal hell.

I let him down when he needed me.

I was supposed to drive Eden home. Instead, I took off in the opposite direction to the airport and left her in the incompetent hands of her boyfriend.

I never blamed Coach for cutting off all contact with me. I deserved his silence.

"I can't remember the last time I danced that much." Eden tosses her purse on a chair in my living room as I lock the door behind us. "Thank you for taking me there."

Scrubbing my hand over the back of my neck, I look over

at the bottle of scotch on my home bar. "Can I get you a drink?"

Her gaze follows mine. "A glass of cold water would be perfect."

No. She's fucking perfect.

She talked non-stop in the taxi on the way here. She loved the band. She enjoyed the wine. She liked Billy even though her interaction with him was limited to a couple of minutes.

I want to take her back there, but we're due in court again in a few days.

Depending on what she's planning on her end, the case should move quickly.

She could be on a flight back to Buffalo within the next two weeks.

I knew going into this that it would run its course, but I need more time.

I stalk into the kitchen and pull a pitcher filled with filtered water out. I fill a tall glass to the brim.

She's studying the pictures on the mantle of the fireplace when I walk back in.

"Ansley is still as gorgeous as ever."

She's right. My older sister is one of the most beautiful women I know. It's not just her striking features. Her heart is made of gold.

She's a mom to three, a wife, and a teacher.

Her students are curious seven-year-olds. She's never short of a story or two when we talk.

Eden's finger trails over the picture of Ansley and me. It was taken last winter in Hawaii. My sister was there with her family because her husband had business on the big island over the holidays.

I made it my business to be there to see them.

Overall, the trip was everything I hoped it would be. I left with good memories, a tan, and a promise from Ansley that she'd find her way to Manhattan when she needs a weekend break from life in Houston.

It hasn't happened yet, but my door is always open for her.

Eden takes the glass of water. "Thank you for this."

I watch her throat work on a swallow. As much as I want my dick back in her mouth, I want to taste her more.

"Take off your clothes."

Her gaze skims my face. "Not so fast. We have a matter to discuss."

The only thing I want to discuss is how badly I need her naked. "What matter?"

She places the empty glass on the mantle. "Your jersey. We need to talk terms if you want it back."

She can keep the damn thing. It's a piece of another life that I'm not sure I want to remember.

I play along because she's smiling like she's holding the pot of gold at the end of a rainbow. "I'm open to an offer. What do you propose?"

She rakes me from head-to-toe, and there's zero chance that I'm reading the look in her eyes wrong. She wants me. She fucking wants me as desperately as I want her.

"I want to undress you."

Her voice is bold and clear. There's no room for misunderstanding.

I hold both my arms out to the side. "Have at it."

Her fingers skim the bottom hem of my sweater. "It's just a starting point. It doesn't mean that I'll bring the jersey back."

"Understood." I glance down at her hands. "Do I get to undress you once my ass is bare?"

Her head shakes slowly. "No. I'll undress myself."

"While I watch?" My brows perk in anticipation of that scene unfolding in front of me.

Her voice drops along with her gaze. "While you touch yourself."

I take a half-step closer to give her easier access to my belt and the zipper of my jeans. "While I stroke my cock?"

She lifts her chin until our eyes meet. "You did it the other night. It was really hot."

I found something that turns her on, so I'm all in. "Let's do it."

"But," she stops to chew on her bottom lip.

I want to lean forward and take over, pulling her lip between my teeth, but I stand my ground, even though my cock is as hard as steel. "But what?"

Pink blooms high on her cheeks. "When you're ready to come, I'll take you in my mouth."

I'm ready right fucking now. I drop a hand to the front of my jeans to squeeze my aching dick. "Do it soon, Eden, or I'm going to blow this load in my pants."

Her hands fall to my belt. "We'll negotiate more after I swallow your cum."

Fuck. Just fuck.

Please let me hold it together until her lips are wrapped around my cock.

She takes her time with my clothes, running her hands over the ridges of my abdomen and my biceps.

Once my hand wraps around my cock, I'm almost gone.

I pump again and again as she stands and watches, her gaze never leaving my dick.

"It's so hot in here," she whispers. "I need to do something about that."

My hand works in long, slow strokes as I watch her

undress. Each button of her blouse reveals another inch of her skin.

Her nipples are already perked into tight points when she slides the bra from her body.

I'm captivated with her every movement as the jeans come off followed by the black lace thong that I wish to fuck I was removing with my teeth.

I hiss out her name, "Eden."

That's all it takes to drop her to her knees.

I grab for her hair, fumbling with the long strands as I shove my cock between her pillow-soft lips.

The rush of desire is instant, violent, and almost too much.

I close my eyes against the onslaught and come hard, chanting her name as I empty every last drop into her.

CHAPTER TWENTY-SEVEN

Eden

WORDS CAN'T DESCRIBE the pleasure that pulses through me when Dylan sinks his thick cock into my pussy.

I tremble around him, wishing that I could feel him without a condom.

Flesh-to-flesh. Our raw desire not hindered by the latex that separates us now.

I moan because it's that good. It's so good.

I've never been with a man who knew how to fuck like this.

Dylan reaches beneath me to cradle my ass cheek in his hand. He tilts me up until the wide head of his cock hits that spot inside of me.

I knew it existed, but it wasn't until the other night, in this bed, that I finally understood what it felt like to be with a man who could use his body to really and truly pleasure a woman.

I come apart when his teeth bear down on my shoulder.

My sex ripples around him, spurring him on.

"Again," he whispers against the shell of my ear. "I want you to come again."

I whimper because I'm still falling from the high of my climax. "I can't."

He slides in and out slowly. "Your cunt says otherwise. You're so wet. You need more."

He's so raw and uninhibited. He doesn't mask his need behind the pretense of flowery compliments or token terms of endearment.

His words are a reflection of his wants.

"On top," I murmur as he plunges deeper.

"Fuck yes," he answers with a flip of our bodies.

I whine when his cock slides out of me. "Please."

He settles on his back in the middle of the bed. His hand is wrapped around the root of his erection. "Ride me, Eden. Take what you want."

I crawl over him, sliding him inside of me. It's so deep that tears well in the corners of my eyes. "It's too much."

"Shh, it's good." His voice soothes, just as his hands stroke my thighs. "Take it slow. Set the pace. Use me to get yourself off."

I lean down to press my lips to his, whispering back what he said to me. "It's good."

"So fucking good." He deepens the kiss with a lash of his tongue against mine. "Fuck me."

I move my body slowly, adjusting to his thickness. I've never felt this full, or this alive.

I slide my hands over his muscular chest until I'm sitting atop him with his cock buried so deep inside of me that the sharp bite of pain is cloaked in pure pleasure.

"You're the most beautiful thing I've ever seen." His voice is gravelly. "Jesus, look at you."

I look down into the face of the man I'm falling so fast and so hard for.

"Look at you," I repeat back before I close my eyes and take what I need.

———

GLANCING DOWN AT ME, Dylan ties off the condom and tosses it in a wastebasket next to the bed.

His bedroom is set up for ease of pleasure.

Condoms sit in full view. A box of tissues is on the other nightstand beside a lamp that is partially shielding a tube of lube.

The wastebasket is within reach, and I'm guessing emptied every morning.

Dylan Colt was made for fucking.

I know because I just experienced it first hand. Or my pussy did. The ache deep within it will remind me of him for at least the next few days.

I'm still sore from our last time.

"What's the next step in our negotiation?" Dylan runs his hand over his semi-hard cock.

I roll to my side. "Not what you think."

His brows perk. "What do I think?"

"It involves my body."

"I can go another round." He looks down at his erection. He's completely hard. "Here's my proposal."

I fight off a smile. "I can't wait to hear this."

"I fuck you twice a day for a year, and in exchange at the end of that time, we revisit the idea of you returning the jersey. I need a caveat in there about eating you. I retain the right to do that in addition to the twice daily fucking."

My smile falls. "Dylan, we…"

"We can't because Buffalo is on the horizon." He nods. "I know."

The moment feels awkward, so I swing my legs over the side of the bed. "I propose you give me back my blouse and skirt in exchange for the return of your jersey the next time we see each other."

He rakes me as I stand. "When will that be? Tomorrow?"

It's tomorrow already. It's nearing two a.m., and I need to go.

"I can't tomorrow." I fold my hands together in front of me.

"Why not?" he asks, rounding the bed until he's in front of me.

I tell him the truth. "I'm working."

"On the Alcester case?"

"Kurt asked me to help with another client," I say. "I'm going to handle some of that tomorrow."

"On Sunday?"

I laugh. "You work on Sundays too."

His hands reach for mine. "I'll take tomorrow off if you do."

I glance down at our fingers woven together. It's so comfortable to touch him. Everything feels like it fits perfectly together. "I need to work."

Resignation floats over his expression. "You're taking off now, aren't you?"

"I am." I don't explain beyond that.

"I'll get dressed and take you back to Noelle's place."

I squeeze his hands in mine. "I know how to get there."

"Understood." Leaning forward, he kisses me softly. "I'll grab your skirt and blouse."

"Dylan," I say his name just as he drops my hands. "Tonight was incredible. It was everything to me."

His hand moves to cup my cheek. "To me too, Eden. Thank you for all of it. I mean it."

I know he does. I see it in his eyes.

I don't protest when he takes a step toward his walk-in closet. I watch him as he moves away from me, knowing that soon we'll be walking away from each other for good.

CHAPTER TWENTY-EIGHT

DYLAN

I GLANCE at the clock before I swing open the door to my apartment. It's mid-afternoon on Sunday. I know it's not Eden. She has work on her plate today. I checked in with her late this morning via text.

She told me she'd be tied up today and tomorrow.

I'm looking at a full schedule for most of the week. There's a good chance that the next time I see Eden, we'll be standing in Judge Mycella's courtroom.

I swing open the door because I know whoever is standing on the other side made it past the doorman.

I didn't order food in, so it's someone with a face familiar enough that the doorman didn't view their presence as deserving of a heads-up phone call to me.

"Colt," Barrett greets me with a nod of his head. "Let me in."

I step aside to give him room to pass. "What the hell are you doing here?"

"It's good to see you too, bastard." He drops his duffel bag and a briefcase at my feet. "What's going on in your world?"

I slam the door shut and turn to face him.

"I'm about to go out for a run."

He takes in the black shorts and white T-shirt I'm wearing. "Hold up on that. We need to talk."

I continue the leg stretches I started before he showed up unannounced. "Let's start with why you're here with an overnight bag. Did I miss the text where I invited you for a visit?"

He shoves his hands into the front pocket of his jeans. "You missed a few phone calls. I was worried about my little buddy."

I laugh aloud. "Since when am I your little buddy?"

"Stroll down memory lane with me." He walks to the couch, planting himself in the middle of it. "I was taller than you when we were twelve. If I recall correctly, you were my little buddy for six months give or take a week."

He'll never let me live that down.

I caught up in height and weight during summer break, but Barrett refuses to let it go.

"Why are you in New York?" I settle back on the heels of my running shoes.

"I thought I'd drop in on my way to London." He pats his thigh. "I'm looking for an update on you and Eden Conrad. Anything new to report on that front?"

"You're going to London?" Deflection never works with Barrett, but there's no harm in trying.

He nods. "I fly out early tomorrow. You're going to tell me what you and Eden have been up to since I left you in her very capable hands."

"We've hung out." I try to keep my voice level.

"Hung out?" He pops both brows. "Is that a polite way to say you've been fucking?"

"It's more than that," I correct him. "We've gone out for dinner. We went dancing."

"You're dating Eden?" He cracks a wide grin. "Look at you acting like a stand-up guy. I'm proud of you for keeping your dick on a leash."

I move to take a seat on a chair across from him. Coach Conrad was an influential force in Barrett's life too. He was the one who broke the bad news to my best friend that an athletic scholarship wasn't in the cards for him.

Barrett took the news like a champ.

He thanked Coach for his honesty and then got drunk on cheap beer.

"I need to tell you something." I edge into the conversation slowly. "It's about Eden."

Curiosity draws his body forward. He rests his elbows on his knees. "What?"

I scratch the back of my neck. There's no easy way to do it, so I come right out with it. "Coach Conrad died three years ago. He's gone."

The look on his face mirrors the one I know was on mine last night.

I go on, "It was cancer."

Barrett's head drops into his hands. "Dammit. Life's not fair. He was the best. You know he was the best."

"I know." I exhale on a sigh. "I was as surprised as you are."

He looks up at me. "How did Eden handle that on her own? Was she on her own when it happened?"

I didn't bother to ask, because she made it damn clear that talking about Clark is off limits. "I don't know. She didn't say."

"Coach had our backs." He pats his thigh. "He looked out for us at every turn. We should have been there to say goodbye to him."

I can't argue with that, so I don't. "I know it."

"I should talk to Eden." He looks at my phone on the coffee table. "Give me her number so I can text her. I need to tell her I'm sorry."

Shaking my head, I lean back in my chair. "I'll tell her that you're sorry when the time is right. It's painful for her to talk about it."

"Whatever you think is best, Colt. You know her better than I ever have."

I can't say that I do. I want to, but time is ticking on my relationship with Eden. The clock is about to run out, and when it does, I'll become a memory from her past again.

CHAPTER TWENTY-NINE

EDEN

FRUSTRATION BROUGHT me to the offices of Kent & Colt.

The court clerk called me thirty minutes ago to tell me that the Alcester case was set back another ten days at the request of Judge Mycella.

I noticed the rapport between Dylan and the judge.

They referred to each other by their first names during our sidebar. It's evident that they have a connection outside the courtroom.

This unexpected delay is his doing. It has to be.

He knows that my client wants this case wrapped up as soon as possible. Prolonging the proceedings is an amateur tactic that some lawyers resort to when they want the other side to settle.

It won't work with me.

I spoke to Troy Alcester right before I left my office.

I assured him that I'd do everything in my power to get the divorce finalized as quickly as possible.

His concern isn't for himself. Troy wants his two daughters to have balance again. They've been stuck in the push and pull between their parents for months.

I walk toward the reception desk in the lavish office that Dylan shares with his partner Griffin Kent.

I did my due diligence once I realized that Dylan was my opposing counsel.

He set up this practice right out of law school with Griffin.

The reception area is decorated beautifully. It's an elegant space. Kurt's offices aren't as lavish, but he hasn't updated the flooring or the paint on the walls in the last decade.

"Can I help you?" A blond haired man wearing a black suit pops up from around a corner.

I glance over at the empty reception desk. "I'm here to see Dylan Colt."

The man rushes toward me, his gaze on the phone in his hand. "I'm Gunner. I'm Mr. Colt's assistant. He doesn't have a meeting scheduled for the next two hours."

Of course, he doesn't. It's noon.

He must be off somewhere enjoying a long, leisurely lunch.

"I'll set you up an appointment for next week. Or if you prefer I can tell him that you stopped by." Gunner stands directly in front of me. "If you give me your name and number, one of us will be in touch."

Dylan's assistant runs interference like his life depends on it.

"My name is Eden Conrad."

His gaze drops to my wrist and the watch I always wear.

Something has shifted in his expression when he locks eyes with me again. "Come with me, Ms. Conrad."

I don't question where we're going. I follow Gunner down a long corridor. A few people come in and out of offices as we pass. All of them smile at me and offer quiet, "hellos."

Dylan's staff is polite and well dressed.

I'm impressed by what he's built here.

Gunner slows as we approach the closed door of an office at the end of the corridor.

He knocks softly before he swings the door open.

"Jesus Christ, Gunner," Dylan's voice booms through the corridor. "You're supposed to wait for me to tell you to come in. Get lost."

I can't help but laugh.

"Hold on," Dylan's voice is louder. "I know that laugh."

Gunner takes a step back as his boss appears in the doorway of his office dressed in a light gray suit and blue tie.

"Look at what we have here." He rakes me over. "To what do I owe this pleasure?"

———

"YOU LOOK BEAUTIFUL TODAY, EDEN." Dylan flashes me a grin as he takes a seat on a brown leather couch in his office.

He sent Gunner on his way before he closed and locked the door to his office.

I don't know what he thinks will happen between the two of us, but it's not going to involve me taking off my navy blue dress.

I came to talk business.

"Why aren't we going back to court this week?" I stand in front of him, propping one hand on my hip.

He leans back on the couch, crossing his legs. "You got a call from Judge Mycella's clerk."

"Peggy's clerk," I say with a smirk. "I know you two are friends."

He fights back a smile. "That's not a crime."

"I'm not falling for your tactics." I punch my hip out even more. "Troy won't settle, Dylan. Your client's terms are completely unreasonable."

"Your client fucked my client over." He exhales in a rush. "As much as I'd like to take credit for the delay, I had nothing to do with it."

Studying his face, I narrow my eyes. I can't tell if he's being serious or not. "Why the delay?"

"Did the clerk not explain that there was a scheduling conflict?"

My shoulders stiffen.

The clerk did explain that Judge Mycella had a conflict that required the rescheduling of a few upcoming cases on the docket. I thought that was a cover for Dylan manipulating things in his favor.

"I play by the rules." Dylan pats the couch next to him. "Come sit down. Let's talk about this."

I shake my head. "You'll try and kiss me."

That perks both his dark brows. "You'll let me kiss you."

I take a step back. "It's not a good idea."

"Why not?"

"You know why." I grab the strap of the purse slung over my shoulder. "A kiss will lead to more."

"My face between your legs?" His gaze drops to the skirt of my dress.

A knock at the door draws him to his feet. "Give me a second. I need to fire my assistant."

My hand jumps to my mouth to cover it as I let out a giggle. "You wouldn't fire him for knocking."

He shoots me a quick wink. "Don't move. I'll be right back."

I turn to watch as he opens the door. Standing on the other side is a tall man with brown hair. He looks at Dylan before his gaze lands on my face.

"You're Eden Conrad," he says quietly.

Dylan blocks the doorframe with his body. "I'm busy, Griffin. "

"We have a situation." His eyes scan Dylan's face. "It involves one of your cases."

"It can wait," Dylan insists with a glance back over his shoulder at me.

"It can't." He pauses before he lowers his voice. "Trudy Alcester is here. She's in my office. She'd like a word."

CHAPTER THIRTY

DYLAN

TRUDY IS as frustrated by the delay in her divorce proceedings as Eden is. I didn't call and break that bad news to my client because I planned on handling that in person later today.

Her estranged husband phoned her to tell her all about it.

That's what brought her to my office.

She wanted to know why Troy was in the loop, and she wasn't.

I give Eden credit for keeping her client informed. I wish she hadn't beaten me to the punch.

I calmed Trudy down, assured her that we'd have our day in court soon, and sent her on her way.

"Dylan!"

I turn at the sound of my partner's voice as I enter the lobby of our building.

I went for a coffee run after my short meeting with Trudy.

I briefly toyed with the idea of picking up a coffee for Eden and dropping by her office, but I decided against it.

She left in a hurry after Griffin told me Trudy was waiting in his office to see me.

Griffin stalks toward me. "Where did you run off to?"

"Gee, dad." I take a sip from the cup in my hand. "Did I miss curfew?"

"Funny." He points at my coffee. "You could have brought your best friend one of those."

"He's in London," I quip. "You can walk the few steps it takes to get to Palla on Fifth. I recommend the dark roast."

His hands disappear into the pockets of his black pants. "What's going on between you and Eden?"

I saw that coming as soon as I opened the door to my office and he caught sight of her.

"Your office door was locked," he goes on. "You only lock it when you're…"

With a woman.

I don't know why he doesn't spit the words out, but they hang there, unsaid.

"Are you asking if I'm fucking her?"

That raises his brow. "I know that you're fucking her. I'm asking how that's going to impact your case."

I don't need to ask him how he knows that I'm sleeping with Eden. He can read me. He's always had that ability.

"The case in on track," I say with confidence.

"Our client's needs come first." He points out with a jab of his finger in the middle of my chest. "I know that you won't lose sight of that."

I look down at his hand. "Trudy will get everything she deserves."

"Good." He taps my shoulder lightly. "You're taking care of you, aren't you?"

One night in college, I confessed to Griffin that I had it bad for a girl named Eden. He knows about the car accident. He's aware that I made the judgment call to walk away and leave Eden with Clark.

"I'm fine, Griffin."

"I'm around if you need me." He straightens the lapels of his jacket. "I'm going to grab a coffee. I'll see you at four at the staff meeting?"

Just like that, we've slid back into business partners.

I know he has my back. Griffin would do almost anything for me, including giving me the space I need to work things out on my own.

"You can count on it."

———

I ASKED Eden to meet me at Calvetti's because I wanted to give her a second chance to enjoy the spaghetti.

I interrupted her dinner the other night when I showed up at her office.

That's why I sent her a text earlier telling her to stop by here at seven, so we can share a meal.

I watch as she walks through the door wearing the blue dress from earlier.

The owner, Marti, approaches her with the greeting she gives almost everyone.

She takes each of her patrons' hands in hers and explains how happy she is that they chose her restaurant out of all the restaurants in the city.

Marti Calvetti is the grandmother of a friend of mine.

She's a sweetheart and without a doubt, the best Italian chef in the five boroughs.

She offered me a hug when I arrived. I gladly took it.

"I found a pretty little lady who knows you," Marti says as she brings Eden to my table. "I told her she was lucky."

I stand and button my suit jacket. "I'm the lucky one."

Marti's gaze moves from my face to Eden's. "There's something special here."

Eden lets out a nervous giggle. "We're fighting each other in court."

Marti tugs on the back of a wooden chair next to the one I've been sitting in. She motions for Eden to take a seat. "You've been doing a lot more than that."

Eden's mouth drops open. "What?"

"He looks at you like you know the secret to his heart." Marti smiles. "You look at him the same way."

Eden doesn't respond, so I step in to change the subject. "I'm starving. What do you recommend tonight, Marti?"

"Sit." She points at my chair. "I'll bring some wine. You'll both have the spaghetti. I made it myself."

CHAPTER THIRTY-ONE

EDEN

I GLANCE over at a family of four enjoying a platter of spaghetti and meatballs. The parents are busy talking while their two young sons slurp up long strands of pasta in a race with one another.

I never had a sibling.

I didn't realize how much I missed that bond until my dad passed away, and I was left alone.

Noelle thinks she fills the role of my sister, but our connection isn't the same as the one she shares with her brother.

"What's on your mind, Eden?" Dylan asks from across the table.

We ate dinner while we traded stories about law school. Dylan went to NYU. I studied at Harvard.

My dad had invested every penny of my mom's life insurance policy in a college fund after her death. I had scholarships in addition to that, so I'm one of the lucky ones who passed the bar without the burden of student debt weighing me down.

Dylan did the same. His parents took care of his education.

"I was thinking about Troy and his daughters." I drag my gaze back to Dylan's face. "He only wants the best for them."

"Their mother is what's best for them," he says without missing a beat. "She'll see to it that they grow up with everything they need."

They need stability and love. They need peace and a sense of belonging.

I met both girls two days ago. Lulu is a spitfire. She's sixteen and set on a career in medicine. Aria is nine. Piano is her passion.

They're lovely and polite, but they're stressed.

I saw it in their eyes when I ran into them and their dad on the sidewalk outside an ice cream shop.

"Have you met them?" I ask. "Have you met the girls?"

He nods. "I stopped by Trudy's one day to deliver some documents. The girls were there."

"They need time with their father."

Dylan sips from the wine glass in front of him. "His work comes first. Everything in his life comes before those two kids including other women. I doubt like hell he knows when his daughters' birthdays are."

His inability to see even a speck of decency in Troy is annoying. I don't consider Trudy perfect, but she's their mom. My goal is not to steal them away from her completely. Troy and I both want equal time for him and his wife.

"I'll fight you hard on this, Dylan," I tell him. "Custody is a big issue for Troy and me."

"I'll win."

The words are curt and final as if he's holding the gavel and taken on the role of the judge.

"You won't win," I shoot back. "I'm going to prove to Judge Mycella that Trudy isn't the better parent."

"I'd like to see you try." He leans back in his chair.

I don't know if it's the frustrations of the case being put over for another ten days or if I'm annoyed with Dylan's callous attitude about the custodial rights of my client, but I've had my fill of spaghetti and my dinner partner.

"We'll work this out in the courtroom." I push away from the table.

Dylan's hand is on my wrist before I can stand. "Where are you going?"

"To Noelle's." I tug my arm free. "I need to pack."

By the time I'm up on my feet, Dylan is too. He edges closer to me, but I ward him off with a hand in the air.

"You're packing? Why?"

"I'm flying to Buffalo early tomorrow." I shoulder my bag. "I have work there that I need to take care of."

He steps closer. His breath skirts over my cheek when he leans down. "I'll go with you. You can bring your things to my place. I'll take you to the airport in the morning."

"I'm staying at Noelle's tonight." I look into his eyes.

"Don't let the Alcester case impact this." His finger circles the air between us. "That's business, Eden. This is…"

"Complicated," I interrupt. "I need to focus on Buffalo for a few days."

"When will you be back?" Frustration edges his tone.

"Soon," I don't offer a specific time even though I know exactly when my flight will land in Manhattan three days from now.

"I'll wait to hear from you." He brushes his lips over my cheek. "Travel safe, Eden. I'm a call away if you need me."

I turn and walk toward the exit of the restaurant.

I do need him. I also need to come to terms with the fact that he'll fight me tooth and nail in court.

I'll confident that I'll win, but I can't help but wonder what it will cost me.

CHAPTER THIRTY-TWO

DYLAN

I HAD to track Eden down.

When her absence dragged into its fourth day, I ached to hear her voice.

I called her cell, Kurt's office, and her office in Buffalo.

She didn't answer, and no one I spoke with gave me any information.

I know that our conversation about custody in the Alcester case caused friction.

Eden's coming at the issue from a different place than I am.

She's walking this earth as an orphan. I have two parents and two stepparents who love me unconditionally.

The loss of her mom left a void in Eden's life that was swallowed up by the pit that was created when her dad died.

She's experienced the absence of parents in a way I never have. I pray I won't for years to come.

I wave her over when she walks into Palla on Fifth.

She looks beautiful dressed in a pair of faded jeans and a patterned blouse.

Her hair is loose and in waves around her shoulders.

It's breathtaking to watch her move. She's graceful and elegant.

"Dylan," she says as she approaches, her face breaking into a wide grin. "It's good to see you."

It's fucking amazing to see her.

I missed her. Jesus, did I miss her.

Everything felt empty in a way it hasn't before. I worked non-stop, and when I couldn't find more to do, I went to the gym.

I didn't even consider taking up the offer of a woman who hit on me when I was on a treadmill.

A month ago, she would have been my type.

Now, my type is the woman standing in front of me.

I scoop her into my arms for a full-on hug. She's petite and perfect. I hold her against me, relishing in the feeling of her hands running a path up and down my back.

When we part, she points at the T-shirt I'm wearing. "You're kidding, right?"

I glance down at the black shirt with the logo of a band I used to listen to in high school. "What?"

"Turn around?" Her finger spins in the air.

I comply, doing a slow turn.

She sighs. "That's a tour shirt from last year. You don't still love their music, do you?"

"Hey, now." I scowl. "Do you see me hating on your taste in music?"

She seats herself in a chair. "I happen to have impeccable taste in music."

"As do I." I lean my hand on the back of my chair.

She gives me a raised brow. "You have questionable taste in music and clothing."

I glance down at the jeans I'm wearing. "What the fuck is wrong with my clothes?"

Narrowing her eyes, she leans back. "The jeans are perfect. I'd lose the shirt."

I drop both hands to the bottom hem of my shirt. "I'll lose it right here."

"You'll get me a coffee first. Then we'll negotiate you losing the shirt."

I swallow. "Deal. It's good to have you back in Manhattan."

Her eyes meet mine. "It's good to be back."

————

AN HOUR LATER, as we settle next to each other on my couch, I look over at Eden. "I didn't handle our conversation about custody in the Alcester case as tactfully as I could have. I fucked that up."

"You did fuck that up."

I like that she calls me on it. I love that she's ready to go head-to-head with me.

"Judge Mycella will determine what is best for the girls." She purses her lips. "You and I are going to discuss what it will take for me to get you out of that T-shirt."

I slip it over my head and toss it behind me in one fell swoop.

She laughs so loud that I can't help but join in.

"Let's talk about what it will take to get you out of that shirt." I look down at the front of the blouse she's wearing. "The jeans too."

She slides to her feet. "This shirt?"

I nod. "What can I do to make you take it off for me?"

Her fingers start to unbutton the blouse. "Does the breakfast for dinner place deliver?"

I fucking love that she calls it that. "They do."

"I want you to order food from there an hour from now."

I'm spellbound as she slips the blouse off, revealing a soft pink bra underneath. "An hour? You're sure?"

Her gaze drops to the front of my jeans. I'm hard and aching. "Two hours?"

"Two hours," I agree with a nod of my head. "What else?"

She slides off her jeans, giving me a glimpse of the black panties she's wearing. "You'll bury the T-shirt in the back of your closet."

"I can't agree to that."

Her bra is off next. Her gorgeous tits bounce as she slides off the panties. "Are you sure you can't agree to it?"

How the fuck am I supposed to talk when I'm looking at the most beautiful woman in the world?

When she steps closer and drops to her knees, I hiss in a deep breath. "Eden."

Her hands race up my thighs to the button of my jeans. "This is my final offer."

I fist my hands in her hair when she slides my zipper down. "You do things to me."

"I'm going to do something special for you." Her lips curve into a sexy smile. "You'll do something for me too."

"Anything," I hiss out.

I'd do anything for her. Anything.

"Take off your pants." She plants a kiss right above the waistband of my boxer briefs.

I look down at the lipstick stain she left behind.

My lips move, but the words don't escape, so I chant them over and over in my mind as I kick off my jeans.

I love you, Eden. I love you, Eden. I've always loved you.

CHAPTER THIRTY-THREE

EDEN

I READ the email I received earlier today for the third time.

Dylan is asleep in his bed. My first instinct was to go back to Noelle's apartment, but I won't.

We had the most incredible night. I don't want tomorrow to come.

I brought him to orgasm with my mouth. He did the same to me. Twice.

After he carried me to his bed, we made love. It was tender in a way it hasn't been before.

He insisted we shower together before he ordered dinner. I've never had a man wash my hair, or slide soap over my most intimate parts.

"Are you working?"

I turn at the sound of Dylan's voice. It's deep and gravelly. There's a hint of sleep in it.

He walks into his living room wearing only boxer briefs.

As he nears me, he lets out a laugh. "Goddammit, woman. I thought you hated that fucking thing."

I tug on the front of his T-shirt. I scooped it off the floor after I slid my panties back on. "I hate the shirt. I love the smell of you."

That stops him mid-step with a hand to the center of his chest. "Eden."

He doesn't need to say more. I motion for him to sit next to me. Once he does, I stretch my bare legs over his lap.

"It's the middle of the night. Work can take a back seat to sleep."

"Maybe in your world." I joke with a pinch of his nipple.

He closes his eyes. "You'll make me hard if you keep that up."

I stare at him. I've never wanted a man this much. I can't imagine I ever will again.

"Were you digging up more imaginary dirt on my client?" He chuckles.

I drop my phone on my lap. "It's not imaginary, but no. This isn't about your client."

He reaches to run a hand over my cheek, chasing away a strand of my hair. "Do you want to talk about it? I'm great at giving legal advice."

I slide my hand over his to bring it closer to my mouth. I nip at his thumb with my teeth. "So am I."

"Again, I'll get harder if you keep that up."

I rub my calf over the growing bulge in his boxers. "You're a beast in bed."

His fingers trail over my chin. "Only for you."

I know that's not true. He was so comfortable when he approached me in the club that first night. He brought me home without thought. He took me into his bed. He's done it countless times before with many women.

"We haven't talked about Buffalo."

I wonder for the briefest of moments if he's going to ask me to consider staying in Manhattan. He joked about it once when we were negotiating the return of his jersey. He hasn't brought it up since.

I haven't either.

I take a deep breath. "What about Buffalo?"

He smiles. "Your trip back. How did that go?"

"It was fine."

"Fine?" He runs his palm over my leg. "Was it good to be home?"

It was lonely. My condo felt empty and too quiet. I took the jersey with me so I could sleep in it. I packed it for the trip back here because I know I'll have to return it before I go home for good.

When that happens, my memories will be all I take with me.

"What do they say about home?" I try to lighten my mood.

"Home is where your favorite T-shirt is." He shoots me a cocky grin. "You already stole one of my shirts. Don't think you're getting out of here with that one too."

"This one you can keep." I tug it over my head, revealing my bare breasts.

His gaze moves across my body to my face. "I want to keep this one forever."

For a split second I think he's talking about me and not the shirt, but he scoops it into his palm and brings it to his face.

Inhaling, he looks over at me. "It has your sweet smell now."

I know our time together is fading, but for tonight, I want

to forget that. All I want is to get lost in the hunger in his eyes and his touch.

He doesn't say a word as I move across the couch to straddle him.

His piercing blue eyes lock on mine, and with a hand in my hair, he pulls me into a deep kiss that leaves me breathless.

Going back to my life in Buffalo and leaving this man behind will be the hardest thing I've ever done.

CHAPTER THIRTY-FOUR

DYLAN

EDEN FINALLY GIVES in and agrees to spend the night with me, and this happens.

What the fuck?

"I'm coming," I say between clenched teeth after another series of raps on my apartment door.

I fell asleep with Eden in my arms less than an hour ago, and now this.

Thankfully, the constant knocking on my door didn't wake her.

It has to be Mrs. Berinco. She lives down the hall. Whenever she has a nightmare, I'm the guy who calms her down with a cup of herbal tea and a story about college.

She's ninety-six-years-old. Her husband died more than twenty years ago. She's lived alone ever since.

"Mrs. Berinco." I swing open the door.

"Is probably fast asleep." Barrett looks me over. "You've been going hard with the crunches. Look at those abs."

I drop my gaze to my bare stomach. I put on a pair of sweatpants before I left my bedroom.

I didn't want to give Mrs. Bernico an eyeful.

"What the hell, Barrett?" I move so he can pass me. "Do you know what time it is?"

He glances at the watch on his wrist. "It's nine a.m. in London."

"Why aren't you there?" I close the door and turn to face him. "Why are you here?"

His attention is on the clothing on the floor. Eden's shirt, her jeans, and her lingerie litter the floor in front of the couch. My jeans and shirt sit in a pile near his feet. "You're not alone."

"I'm not."

That turns him back around. "Eden?"

I nod. "Eden's asleep."

He stalks toward me. "I'm out of here. I should have called first, but you probably wouldn't have picked up."

I huff out a laugh. "I wouldn't have picked up."

"I'm flying out tomorrow afternoon." He adjusts the strap of his duffel bag on his shoulder. "If you want to meet for coffee, give me a call. I'm going to grab a room at the hotel down the street so I can crash."

"Barrett?"

We both turn at the sound of Eden's voice.

She's standing near the hallway. She's wrapped in the blanket from my bed. She looks like an angel with the light filtering in from the window illuminating the side of her face.

"Eden." Barrett raises his hand in a wave. "I'm sorry if I woke you."

"You didn't." She takes a step closer. "I got a call. I need to go."

I push past Barrett so I can get to her. I hear the tremble in her voice. I see the way she's shivering under the blanket.

"What's wrong?" I look down at her face.

Her eyes meet mine. "Kurt had a minor setback. Noelle is upset."

"Is he alright?" I don't consider Kurt a friend, but I respect the man. I want to see him back in the courtroom as soon as possible.

"He's fine." She sets a reassuring hand on my cheek. "Noelle could use a friend right now."

"Do you want me to take you home?"

She leans closer, lowering her voice as her lips sweep over my ear. "I'll be fine. I need my clothes."

"Go back to the bedroom." I kiss her forehead softly. "I'll bring them to you. I'll get a car to take you."

"I ordered an Uber." Her lips brush against mine. "Tonight was special, Dylan."

I can't take my eyes off of her when she turns and goes down the hallway, disappearing into my bedroom.

It was the best night I've ever had. I wish it could play on repeat for the rest of my life.

———

FOUR HOURS LATER, Barrett walks into my living room, showered and wearing jeans and a black dress shirt. He looks rested. I wish I could say the same for me.

I didn't sleep at all after Eden took off last night.

I texted her twenty minutes ago to check in, but I haven't heard back yet.

I hope to hell she's fast asleep.

"You're in love with Eden Conrad," Barrett says, looking at me. "Don't deny it, Colt."

I could. Maybe I should, but why? I am in love with her. I doubt I ever stopped loving her.

"I'm not denying it." I slide a dark blue tie under the collar of my shirt.

"What are you going to do about it?"

I take time with the tie. When it's finally perfect, I look at him again. "Nothing."

"Wrong answer." He takes a step toward me. "You're going to tell her how you feel because you fucked that up fifteen years ago and I'm not letting it happen again."

I huff out a laugh. "You don't have a say in this."

His arms cross his chest. "I sure as hell do. I'm the one who watched you waste time looking for an Eden replacement. You're not falling back into that."

He's right. I'm not. The thought of fucking another woman does nothing for me.

I can't go back to that. I won't get into bed with anyone else.

I want Eden, but her life is in Buffalo and from where I'm standing, she's not looking to add me to the mix there.

"This has an expiry date. We both knew it going in."

"Who had that brilliant idea?" Barrett raises a brow. "You?"

"We both agreed to it." I slide my suit jacket on. "She's heading back home once the case she's working on is settled."

"You can change that." He reaches forward to tug on the lapels of my jacket. "You need to tell her how you feel so she can decide whether Buffalo is home."

"Buffalo is home to her," I reiterate that fact. "She works there. She owns a place there."

"You work in New York. You own a place here. All of that can be changed." His arm waves in the air. "Your argument is weak, Colt. What the hell is really going on here?"

I shove a hand through my hair. "We're having fun until she goes home. It's what we agreed to."

"Don't blow this for a second time." He takes a step back. "You didn't tell her how you felt in high school. This is your chance to right that wrong. Don't let it pass you by."

It's the only wrong I can right, but it's not fair to Eden. If I want a future with her, I need to confess to the past I've kept hidden from her.

I doubt like hell she'll find it in her heart to forgive me for that.

CHAPTER THIRTY-FIVE

EDEN

"I WISH there were two of me," I say to Mrs. Burton. "Buffalo Eden and New York City Eden. The former could use a run right now. The latter wants a cocktail. Decisions. Decisions."

The only response from her is a nudge of her glasses up the bridge of her nose.

Tough crowd.

I know I'm not Kurt Sufford, but you'd think by now she would have warmed up to me just a little bit.

She's been in my office for the past two hours. We're going over the finer details of a case that I told Kurt I'd work on.

He called Noelle this morning to reassure her that he's fine. He had a blood pressure spike last night and ended up back in the hospital for observation.

He's home now, resting and reading over every open case file.

I agreed to close out this one for him since the only issue left to settle is custody of two prized poodles.

I spent the afternoon working out a schedule that will give our client most weekdays and every second weekend with the pups.

Everyone, including the dogs, is happy with the arrangement.

She clears her throat, but that's it. There are no words that follow that.

I'm going to let her off the hook because I need alone time and a martini. I wasn't kidding when I told her that.

"You can go home, Mrs. Burton."

That pops her head up. "I can?"

I shrug. "Yes. Please take the rest of the afternoon off."

She slides forward on the leather chair she's sitting in. "Did I do something wrong?"

I shake my head. "No. Absolutely not. You've been nothing but helpful."

She's been a little off-putting, but that's because I'm not Kurt and I know she's worried about him. As soon as I got to work this morning, she asked me for an update on his condition.

She scratches the side of her neck. "Mr. Sufford doesn't approve of leaving early."

I'm an old family friend, so I know that Kurt has always offered a great deal of latitude to me. I'm not a regular employee. I've tried hard to never take advantage of that.

"I approve of it." I smile across my desk at her. "I want you to take the rest of the day off."

She's on her feet as if she thinks I'll blink my eyes and change my mind. "Maybe I'll see if Mr. Sufford is up for a visit."

It's a testament to how fond she is of her boss. I saw the

picture of Kurt, Thelma, Mrs. Burton, and a man I assume is Mr. Burton on her desk.

I push myself up from my chair, straightening the skirt of my red dress as I rise. "Thank you for all your help today."

Her brows draw together. "There's no need to thank me, dear. It's my job."

I smile.

Dear. It's what my dad always called me. I miss it.

"I'll see you bright and early tomorrow, Ms. Conrad."

"Eden," I say, even though I know she won't call me that.

I've suggested it at least a dozen times since I got to Manhattan. She's always called me Ms. Conrad.

"Thank you for the afternoon off, Eden." A soft smile plays on her lips.

I nod.

Mission accomplished.

———

"IF YOU WEAR that dress to court next week, I'll lose the case."

I laugh. I want to take a step closer and kiss him, but we're in the lobby of Dylan's office building. People are watching us as they pass us by. I assume some of them work for him.

"All it takes is a red dress to defeat you?"

"It's what's in the dress that I'm worried about." He flashes me a smile. "I heard you hammered out a deal for shared custody of the Townsend poodles. That was a steep mountain to climb."

"Good news travels fast in this town." I tilt my head. "Who told you that? I just signed off on the agreement thirty minutes ago."

"Betsy broke the good news to me."

I rub the back of my neck. "Betsy?"

"I saw her at Palla on Fifth." He holds up a large coffee cup. "She seemed extra chipper today."

I stop him before he goes on. "Who is Betsy?"

He narrows his eyes. "You're kidding, right?"

I shrug both shoulders. I'm completely and utterly lost. "I'm serious."

He leans forward until he's so close that his breath slides over my ear. "I'll give you a clue, counselor."

I pull back just a touch so I can look into his eyes. "What's the clue?"

"It comes at a price."

Of course, it does. "Is the price open for negotiation?"

The corners of his lips curve up. "Isn't it always?"

I'm tempted to suggest that we take our negotiation to his bedroom, but I like the game we're playing.

Amusement dances in his eyes. "I'm open to offers."

I gaze down at the watch on my wrist. "I have thirty minutes right now. Do what you will to me in your office. Or I'll do you. Your choice."

His hand leaps to mine. "I'll do you."

I follow behind him as he leads me through the lobby toward the bank of elevators. "Who is Betsy? What's the clue?"

He stabs the elevator call button three times. "Jesus, hurry the fuck up."

I look around to see if anyone is noticing his haste and the growing bulge in his suit pants.

"Keep it together, Colt," I whisper.

"I don't have condoms in my office, so it's fingers or mouth. You choose." He glides his index finger over his bottom lip.

"Both," I answer. "I want both."

He looks me over from head-to-toe. "Done."

The elevator doors pop open. We both step aside to let three people exit. Once we're on board, along with two older men, he presses the button for the floor that houses his offices.

I tap Dylan on the shoulder, luring his gaze to meet mine.

A smile plays on his mouth as he cocks a dark brow in question.

"Who is Betsy?" I ask quietly.

"I said I'd give you a clue." His eyes narrow. "You gave her the afternoon off."

"Mrs. Burton," I mutter to myself.

Why am I not surprised that he knows her first name?

"Betsy Burton. She's Kurt's assistant. I owe her a debt of gratitude."

I already know the answer, but still, I ask the obvious question so that I can hear him say the words. "Why do you owe her?"

He leans so close to me that his full lips press against the shell of my ear. "Because I get a taste of you in the middle of my day."

I close my eyes as a shiver runs through me. "Dylan."

"Hold that thought." His hand reaches behind me to cup my ass. "And that moan."

The elevator dings its arrival on Dylan's floor.

"I'm about to make you come." His voice is barely audible, but I hear every syllable and feel his desire in the way his hand slides over my ass to the center of my back.

"This way, Ms. Conrad." He directs me out of the elevator, shooting a look back over his shoulder at the men still on the lift. "Enjoy the rest of your afternoon, gentlemen. I know I will."

CHAPTER THIRTY-SIX

DYLAN

I CUP my hands over my mouth, inhaling the sweet fragrance of Eden.

This was a treat that I didn't see coming. By treat, I mean her coming on my face on the couch here in my office.

I look over to where she's adjusting the front of her dress.

No one would suspect that she just had an orgasm unless they noticed the thin sheen of sweat that dots the skin above her top lip or the pink hue of her cheeks.

"I didn't come here for that." She points out. "I came to talk about business."

"I don't know of a better way to start a business meeting."

She shakes her head. "How many business meetings have you started that way?"

Her expression shifts. The playfulness that was in her eyes is replaced with concern.

"Do you really want me to answer that?" I ask.

Her eyes flit over my face. "Actually, yes. I'm curious."

I slip my suit jacket back on. I tossed it onto my desk when I crawled between her legs.

"Today was the first time," I answer honestly.

I had a brief fling with one of our former receptionists months ago. I recognized it as a mistake right away. It was the first and only time I mixed business with pleasure until now.

"You haven't slept with other attorneys?" she scoffs. "I find that hard to believe."

I close my eyes briefly, wondering how the fuck this came up right after the encounter we just had.

"You didn't ask me about other attorneys. You asked me whether I had fucked anyone I was working with."

Realization drops her gaze to the floor.

New York is a big town, but my time is limited. If I'm not at a club looking for a woman to spend the night with, I fall back on women I've already slept with.

It's rare, but it does happen.

Two of the women I met in law school kept in touch. I fucked one for a month years ago. We mutually agreed it wasn't working. I haven't heard from her since.

The other woman stepped back into my life three years after we both passed the bar. She was looking for a job. I was out for a good time.

I got what I wanted. She did too, but not in terms of employment.

That lasted all of two weeks before she ran back to her ex.

"Do you still see them?" Hesitation edges her words. "It's not that it matters. I'm just curious."

She's not innocent. She mentioned in passing that she slept with a colleague.

"I don't." I round my desk. "You told me that you've

mixed business with pleasure. That was with someone you work with? A lawyer?"

She nods in silence.

"I take it that's over now?"

Confirmation never hurt anyone, especially someone who is in love with the person he's questioning.

"Over?"

I search her face, trying to determine if she's serious. "O.V.E.R. Over. It's a straightforward word. Is your relationship with your colleague over?"

"Our sexual relationship is over for now."

What the actual fuck?

I lean forward, bracing both palms on the top of my desk. "And that means?"

"We still work together."

I'm a master of masking surprise, so I slip on my best stoic expression and carry forward, as I do every fucking day in court.

Except, I'm not in court.

I'm in my office with the woman I'm crazy about; the same woman I just ate to an orgasm.

"Do you still fuck each other?"

Her hands drop to her hips. "Only when we're on. When we're off, it's hands-off each other."

"On and off?" I question because I'm looking for some clarity here.

"We dated on and off." She explains with a tilt of her finger in the air. "We are off right now. Obviously."

Which leaves the door open for them to be on again?

"Did you see him when you went back to Buffalo?"

She pushes a hand through her long hair, making it even messier. "Of course. We work together."

Whoever the fuck this guy is I hate him, almost as much as I hate Clark Dodson.

I'm a man who needs all available information to process things, so I ask the one question I'm not sure I want an answer to. "How long has this on and off thing been going on?"

She levels her chin to look me straight in the eye. "Three years."

It feels like a punch to my gut.

There's history there. There's enough of something that they feel the pull to get back together over and over again.

"Chet and I haven't been together in months."

"Chet?" I cock a brow. "His name is Chet?"

"Chet Richmond."

I know what I'll be doing the second she's out the door.

Google is almost always a cure-all for curiosity.

Her gaze drops to her wrist and the watch she left at my place the first night we fucked. That was before I realized who she was or that some jerk named Chet Richmond has been in and out of her bed for the past three years.

"I have a meeting I need to get to." She moves to pick up her tote bag.

I nod. I won't try and keep her. I'm going to seek out a beer and the life history of Chet Richmond, Esquire.

"Oh." She flips her hair over her shoulder and fuck me, she's so goddamn beautiful.

"Oh?" I repeat back.

"I came here for a reason." She sighs. "It's about the Alcester case. We don't have time to get into it now, but since I'm here, I do have a question for you."

"Ask away."

"Have you seen my earring?" She tugs on her right ear lobe.

I glance at the diamond studs in her ears. I point at the one she's touching. "There it is."

A smile parts her lips. "It's a silver hoop. I left my watch at your place, so I was hoping I did the same with my earring."

I didn't notice it when I was getting ready for work this morning, but I wasn't on the look-out for it either.

"I'll check around."

"I have something to negotiate for it." Her tongue drags over her lower lip.

My cock hardens because there's no way in hell that it can't when she's tempting me.

"I have something from high school that I think you'll be happy to see."

That's impossible. She's the only memory of my past that I want to see.

I play along because she's enjoying the hell out of this. "What is it?"

"You find the earring, and I'll give you a clue."

A smile ghosts my mouth. "I'll do my best."

My office phone rings, even though I told Gunner to hold all calls.

"That's my cue to go." She takes a step toward me but stops herself before she takes another.

"I'll walk you to the elevator."

She glances at my phone. "Answer that. I know the way out."

I ignore the phone, so I can watch her walk away.

As curious as I am about what she's holding onto from my past, I'm focused on something else.

I want to know who the hell Chet Richmond is and when he was last "on" the woman I love.

CHAPTER THIRTY-SEVEN

EDEN

MY PHONE CHIMES with the arrival of another email.

I'm expecting a client in Buffalo to touch base, but that's not what this email is about.

I don't have to open it to know what it says. It's a follow-up to an email from the other day. An email I have yet to respond to.

I exit the mail app on my phone and toss it next to me on the couch.

Noelle taps me on the shoulder from behind. "Do you want dessert?"

I pat my stomach through the white T-shirt I'm wearing. "I'm stuffed. I'm glad I'm wearing leggings. I need to go run ten miles to work off that dinner."

She playfully tugs on my ponytail. "I'm going to take that as a compliment."

I bend my neck back to look up at her. "As you should.

Those fish tacos were delicious. Why are you a doctor and not a chef?"

She moves around the couch to take a seat next to me. "I'm both."

"How's your dad?" I ask for the first time since I got home from work.

Noelle was already here, dressed in a pair of pajamas. Her sleep schedule has been messed up since Kurt's surgery.

Her worry over that and her workload has taken its toll.

I offered to cook dinner, but she insisted that I relax while she handled it.

Cooking is an outlet for her. It helps ease her anxiety. The bonus is that she's good at it.

"Better." She heaves a sigh of relief. "His doctor has advised him to cut his time at work in half. She told him that it would be a good idea to consider retirement sometime soon."

Kurt's nearing seventy. Vacations have taken a backseat to work for most of his life.

I chime in even though I'm not immediate family. "I think he should retire. He's worked hard for a very long time."

"Don't tell him that." She jabs a finger into my side. "You know how he is about his age."

I know. He tells anyone who will listen that he's fifty-five. The graying hair on his head and the lines of wisdom around his eyes and mouth tell a different tale.

I put a finger over my lips. "These are sealed tight."

"It would work to our benefit if he did retire." She props a yellow throw pillow between her head and the couch. Closing her eyes, she goes on, "Dad retiring would mean that the firm would need someone special to step into his shoes."

"He has a long list of potential candidates in his office."

Her eyes pop open. "I see the best of the best in front of me."

I admit that since I came to Manhattan, I've imagined what it would be like to live here full-time. This city has an appeal that I can't deny. The energy is different here. There's a pulse that Buffalo doesn't offer me.

"Promise me one thing, Eden."

"I'll promise you anything if you promise me you'll go to bed as soon as we've finished this conversation." I rub her knee. "You're drifting off."

"I promise." Her eyelids flutter shut briefly again. "Promise that if my dad does retire, that you'll talk to him about working in New York."

"When your dad retires, I'll sit down with him and talk." I choose each word carefully.

"That's all I ask." She lets out a yawn. "I'm going to bed. Don't touch the dishes."

I won't promise that. I'll tidy up, do the laundry, and make her a fruit salad for breakfast tomorrow before I go to bed.

"Sweet dreams, Noelle," I call after her as she takes off down the hallway to her bedroom.

I glance down at my phone when it pings a notification of a new text message.

I scoop it into my palm.

Dylan: I'm headed home to start a search for that earring.

It's almost nine. I wait for a beat to see if he'll send a follow-up message.

Dylan: You're more than welcome to help.

I have a case file to read over after I take care of things around here.

Eden: I can't tonight, but I have faith in you.

His reply comes quickly.

Dylan: Big plans?

My fingers fly over the phone's screen before I press send again.

Eden: Work and sleep.

Dylan: Until tomorrow then.

Eden: Goodnight.

I close the messaging app and open the email app.

I stare at the unread email before I click the envelope to open it. I read every word before I hit reply.

I press send after typing out three short words: I'll be there.

CHAPTER THIRTY-EIGHT

Dylan

I SPENT most of the morning with a client who is nearing the finish line on his seventh divorce.

I sat in his office uptown and listened when he went on about the unflattering traits of his estranged wife. I didn't interrupt him when he repeatedly brought up the names of his fifth and sixth ex-wives.

He needs a chart just to keep of what he doesn't like about the women he once loved enough to marry.

After two hours of that, I cut in to tell him that I had all the information I needed.

What I really had was zero patience left.

I'm good at what I do, but some cases wear on me.

That's one of them.

He'll never take my advice not to get married again. I'm here the next time he needs me. I'm betting that will be within the next eighteen months.

"Mr. Colt," Gunner says my name just as he raps his knuckles against the doorframe of my office.

I didn't jump this time because I heard him coming down the corridor. I threatened to buy bells for his shoelaces if he didn't start warning me of his impending arrival.

Since then, he's become heavy-footed; stomping out his steps to alert me that he's on his way to interrupt my day.

"What is it?" I ask back in a clipped tone.

"Is something bothering you, sir?"

Someone is bothering me. On any other day, Gunner would be that someone, but today the title belongs to Chet Richmond.

I Googled the hell out of him last night.

I was up to the wee hours, reading everything I could find on the model-turned lawyer.

Who gives up a career modeling next to some of the world's most beautiful women to go to law school?

Chet Richmond does.

He also volunteers at a soup kitchen in Buffalo, runs marathons, and builds birdhouses in his spare time.

I made up that last one, but I wouldn't be surprised if there's an image online of him with a hammer in his hand.

There are thousands of images of Chet for public consumption.

Long-haired Chet. Short-haired Chet. Chet in a speedo. Chet in a thousand dollar suit.

Misery loves company when you're drunk on beer and staring at the guy who has been rolling in and out of bed with the woman you can't stop thinking about.

Gunner steps into my office, closing the door behind him. "Mr. Colt? Sir? I can help."

I highly doubt that.

"Is it about Ms. Conrad?" Gunner oversteps that boundary with ease.

"It's none of your business." I halt him in place with a hand in the air.

He stops. "You've been ignoring your calls since you got back from your meeting. You haven't read any of your emails this morning. If you need to talk, I have two ears."

"I appreciate the effort, Gunner, but we'll never be friends."

The corners of his mouth dip into a frown. I almost feel bad, but that passes within a half a second. I pay him too well to feel sorry for him.

He clears his throat. "Talking always beats sulking."

"Firing your assistant beats listening to him quote bullshit."

He laughs. "Mrs. Alcester needs a word, sir. She's called twice already today."

Of course, she needs a word. We're due back in court days from now.

"Get her on the phone." I point at my office door. "Do it from your desk."

"Will do."

I wait for him to take a step, but he stays in place, a grin plastered on his mouth.

"Now would be the time to get it done, Gunner."

"Are you busy later?" He shuffles his feet on the floor. "I thought maybe we could go for pizza. My treat."

I created a monster with a couple of slices of pepperoni and a cheap bottle of beer.

I offer him a compromise. "We'll do lunch. One hour. Your treat and no beer."

"I'll meet you at the elevator at noon sharp."

"I'll get there when I get there," I counter. "Go call Mrs. Alcester, and if Ms. Conrad calls…"

"I'll put her right through, sir." He smiles. "That goes without saying."

———

THE PIZZA WAS DELICIOUS. The company was bearable.

I sent Gunner back to the office ten minutes ago to handle an email from a client that requires an immediate response.

I took care of lunch because it's a business expense. Gunner saw fit to view it through a friendship lens, but that's on him.

I'm outside the restaurant now under the warming early afternoon sun.

Going back to the office is a must, but I take a second to do something before I hit the pavement for the walk back.

I scoop the silver hoop earring out of my pocket, place it my palm, and snap a quick picture of it.

Attaching it to a text, I send it to Eden with a short message.

Dylan: Look what I have.

I start down the sidewalk, hoping she'll respond soon.

I look down when my phone pings in my hand.

Eden: Yay! I love that earring.

Walking and texting is a dangerous endeavor in Manhattan, but a man has to live on the edge sometimes.

Dylan: It's available for pick-up at my place tonight.

Her response arrives just as I'm crossing the street.

Eden: Perfect! I'll bring that something special from high school I told you about.

Dylan: You're the only something special from high school I care about.

My thumb hovers over the send button, but Eden beats me to the punch.

Eden: I'm running into a meeting. I'll see you at eight!

I delete every word of the message I was going to send her before I pocket my phone.

The expiry date we put on this is inching ever closer. My time is running out, and I'm not ready for that. I need to make a move before it's too late.

CHAPTER THIRTY-NINE

DYLAN

EDEN ARRIVED RIGHT ON TIME.

I went down to the lobby to greet her. I exited the elevator at five to eight but hung back when I noticed her standing to the side talking on her cell.

She was nodding her head. A wide smile bloomed on her mouth for the person on the other end of that call.

I watched her twirl in a circle after she dropped her phone in her purse. She smoothed her hand over the skirt of the light blue sundress she's wearing.

That's when she noticed me.

With a wave of her hand, she walked over and greeted me with a soft kiss to the mouth.

It literally made my knees shake.

We're in my apartment now. She's on the couch with her legs crossed and a smile on her face. I assume that has to do with the 'something special' from high school that she's going to spring on me.

"Did you just get home from work?" She points at the dark blue trousers and white button-down shirt I'm wearing.

The sleeves of the shirt are rolled up, but a tie still hangs around my neck.

Work kept me in my office until thirty minutes ago. I had just enough time to come up here, lose my suit jacket, and take a shot of scotch before I rode the elevator back down to meet her.

"I don't do nine-to-five like some attorneys in this city." I hand her the glass of water she requested after I shut my apartment door.

She takes a sip before placing it down on the coffee table, taking the time to slide a metal coaster underneath it.

"Were you working on a proposal for the Alcester case?" she asks with a sly smile.

I take a seat next to her. "Not a chance."

"So we're actually going to do this?" Her brows inch up.

I start loosening my tie. "You're eager, but I'm here to please."

She laughs, swatting my hands away from my neck. "I wasn't talking about sex. I was talking about the case. You want to take this to trial."

"That's where we're headed." I finish up with the tie, tossing it on the coffee table before I work on the top two buttons on my shirt. "If your client is ready to sign off on our financial and custody demands, we can avoid seeing Judge Mycella."

"Your client needs to check herself." Her eyes dart from my face to the skin that's exposed under my shirt. "She's going to regret not taking what's being offered to her."

I don't want to talk business tonight. I had a hell of a day with people chirping in my ear about the person they once walked down the aisle with.

Hatred and vile are a part of the daily when you do what I do for a living, but today was particularly brutal.

I reach into the pocket of my pants and slide out her earring. "Let's talk about what I'm offering you tonight."

She reaches for the earring, but I close my fingers around it before she gets there.

"Dylan," she whines. "Give it to me."

"I want something first."

Her brows pop up. "Right. You want that special thing from high school."

Her hand darts toward her tote bag, but I stop it mid-air when I grab her wrist. "I want you to kiss me."

Her tongue glides over her bottom lip. I lean out, just as she leans closer. Our lips meet in a soft kiss.

I reach for the back of her head to tilt her just right. Her lips part to let me in. Our tongues tangle in an achingly familiar way. The need to take her to bed is strong.

She breaks the kiss because there's no way in hell I will.

"Dylan." My name has never sounded sweeter. "I have something to give you."

I want you. That's all I fucking want.

There's no stopping her, so I watch as she fishes in her tote.

Before I realize what's happening, she places something in my hand.

"You probably thought you'd never see this again. It's going to bring back so many memories." Her voice is edged with delight, as if she's just handed me a treasure I've been hunting down for years.

I look down at the thick silver ring in my hand. It's tarnished, but the crest is unmistakable. I wore this ring after we won the junior state championship. We lost senior year.

On the night we graduated, in all my infinite wisdom, I

slid the ring off and left it on a table at the party before Barrett and I took off for the airport.

It was something a spoiled ass kid would do.

I fit that bill to a tee.

"It's your ring." She traces her fingertip over the crest. "Your name is engraved on the inside of the band."

I stare down at the reminder of the worst night of my life.

"I found it at a party. You must have dropped it." She chuckles. "I picked it up, and it ended up in a box of my things. I brought it back from Buffalo for you."

I swallow hard, finally looking up at her.

"Can you believe you have it back?"

I shake my head. "I can't."

Her hand darts out, palm outstretched. "A deal is a deal, so give me back my earring."

I open my fisted hand and drop the earring into her palm.

"Hey." She playfully punches my bicep. "We just negotiated something and kept our clothes on."

I look back down at the ring. I never thought I'd see this again. It feels like she just handed me a key that opens the door to my past.

All I have to do is use it to start a discussion about the night we graduated.

There's no chance for a future with her, if I don't set the past straight.

CHAPTER FORTY

Eden

I CAN'T TELL if he's happy to see the ring or not.

The expression on his face is unreadable. That's a must for a skilled attorney inside a courtroom. Dylan has mastered it outside as well.

"Try it on," I suggest because I'll do anything to get a smile out of him.

I've held onto that ring for more than fifteen years. When he walked out of the party that we were at on the night we graduated, I saw it on a table.

I knew it was his before I touched it.

I scooped it up, shoving it into the front pocket of the jean cut-offs I was wearing.

The doctors in the ER that night had to cut the shorts off of my body, but they put the ring in a small plastic zippered bag along with my house key.

A nurse handed it to me once I was conscious again.

I waited for Dylan to visit me in the hospital, but he never came.

Once I was discharged, I kept it in my jewelry box, and eventually, that ended up in a cardboard box in the corner of my closet in Buffalo.

"It won't fit." He looks down at it. "My hands are bigger now."

I take the comment and run with it. "You're a perfect example of that saying about men with big hands having big…"

"Cocks," he interrupts me.

"Egos," I say flippantly. "That's bigger now than it was in high school too."

He sets the ring on the coffee table. "You like the size of my ego."

Glancing down at the earring in my hand, I sigh. "I admit I like it. I like a lot of things about you."

"Like what?"

I drop the earring in my bag before I turn to face him. "Your eyes."

He smiles, bringing a dimple to his cheek. "My eyes."

I stare into them. "Before I started at Harvard, my dad and I went to Boston."

"Coach always talked about seeing a Patriots game."

He did talk about that. He never made it there, but we drove past the stadium twice during that visit.

"We took a ferry to Spectacle Island." I sigh, remembering how my dad looked standing on the deck, staring out at the water. He was at peace. It was the first time in years that he finally looked happy. "A woman working at the front desk in the hotel we were staying at in Boston, recommended it."

He takes my hand in his but doesn't say anything.

I go on because it's important for me to tell him. "There is all this beautiful sea glass there. It's everywhere. You're not allowed to take it, but…"

"But you broke that rule." He runs a fingertip over my palm.

I nod. "I was scared I'd get caught, but there was one piece I had to have. I couldn't leave without it."

A soft smile floats over his lips. "What was so special about it?"

I slide my gaze to his face, taking in every feature as if I'm seeing it for the first time. This is what it felt like when I was a teenager looking into his eyes the day I met him.

"Tell me," he urges, bringing my hand to his lips for a soft kiss.

"The sea glass was the color of your eyes," I whisper. "I took it because it reminded me of you."

———

HE KISSES me in a way he never has before.

There's so much tenderness that it brings a tear to my eye.

I swear I feel one slide down his cheek too, but when I try to pull away from the kiss to look, his hands jump to my face, cradling me.

"I need you," he whispers in such a deep, gruff tone that my core clenches.

I reply with only a nod and a stuttered moan.

We're both on our feet before I realize what's happening.

He takes my hand, leading me down the hallway to his bedroom.

The lighting is low. I can't see his face as clearly as I want to, but I can sense what he feels.

Tonight will be different.

My hands slide to the belt of my wrap dress, but he takes over, gently nudging my fingers away.

"Let me, Eden. Please let me."

I don't say anything. Everything I need to say is too much for this moment.

The words have been trapped inside of me for so long that I don't know if I can sort through them enough to make him understand them.

I love him.

I have loved him since the first time he turned around at football practice and locked those beautiful blue eyes on my face.

I lost my heart to him that day on the field.

He slides my dress from my body, growling when he sees what I'm wearing underneath.

It's a light blue bra and panties that I bought just for him.

I stopped at the Liore lingerie store on my way home from work the other day and chose these things because I knew he'd think I was beautiful.

I am beautiful. In his eyes, I'm the most beautiful woman in the world tonight.

In my eyes, I'm a survivor who has fought her way to this moment.

I reach for the buttons of his dress shirt.

His hands leap to mine when he notices how much I'm trembling. I feel as though this is our first time.

Maybe it is. Maybe this is the first time we'll make love with our hearts this open.

He takes over removing his shirt and his pants. His boxer briefs are kicked off and I take in his beautiful, strong, lean body.

His cock is hard. I move to wrap my hand around the root, but he stops me.

"Get on the bed." His voice is edged with a need that I haven't heard before.

I unclasp my bra, slide my panties down, and lower myself onto his bed all while staring at his face.

Everything about him is all I'll ever need, and as he crawls onto the bed next to me, I know that my life will forever be changed after tonight.

CHAPTER FORTY-ONE

DYLAN

SHE SQUIRMS beneath me as I eat her with a hunger I've never felt before.

My mission is simple. I want her to feel a depth of pleasure she hasn't experienced until tonight.

She cries out when I stroke her clit with the tip of my tongue.

"You're teasing me," she whimpers.

I glance up at her body. Her nipples are perked, her tits moving with each undulation of her hips.

One of her hands is covering her face. The other is laced so tightly in my hair that I'm sure she's going to have a few strands left in her palm when I'm done.

"You love it," I growl out the words. "You love this."

"God, so much." She breathes out on a sigh.

I take her swollen clit between my lips and suck.

Her thighs clench, her ass lifts, and I know she's gone.

She's racing to the edge with a heady cry from deep within her.

I grab hold of her hips and ride the wave with her, sucking and licking her through it, until she shudders.

I don't stop.

I don't push for more.

I gently lay kisses over her pussy and the inside of her thighs as her breathing levels.

I want more. I crave more of her, but I stop when I feel her hand loosen in my hair.

Her body goes lax beneath me.

"That was…" she giggles. "I don't know what words to use."

I glance up to see her staring down at me. "You don't need words."

She rests her head back against the pillow. "Good because there are no words."

I rain kisses on her flesh as I crawl up her beautiful body. I stop to circle my tongue over the sensitive skin between her breasts. Whenever I touch it, she moans.

It brings her pleasure so I'll remember it. Always.

When I reach her mouth, I kiss her softly. "Thank you, Eden."

Her eyes widen when I move to sweep a strand of hair from the side of her face. "I'm the one who should be thanking you."

"That's a gift to me." I kiss her again; taking time to breathe her in. "Your pleasure is a gift."

Her bottom lip trembles.

My cock is aching. I'm so hard that all it would take is a brush of her hand against the tip of my dick to make me come.

Feeling her climax under me almost sent me into an

orgasm, but I held back because I want to feel her heat wrapped around me.

"I'll give you five minutes before I fuck you." I take her bottom lip between my teeth, tugging it softly.

Her hand curls around the back of my neck. "Now."

"You'll come again," I say it as much as a promise as a warning.

"I know." Her soft lips curve against mine. "Please."

I'll never deny her my body.

I reach for a condom, sheathing myself with a groan because I'm already so lost to this. I'm already imagining how tight her cunt is.

I slide into her in one smooth stroke. It's so intense that I have to close my eyes to ward off the raw need to give in and fuck with abandon.

I want to savor this.

She brings her hips up to meet mine, sinking me even deeper inside of her. Her hands run a path down my shoulders and arms and back up until they settle on my chest.

I take her in slow strokes at first, giving her time to adjust to the length.

Her body responds with a demand of its own when she clenches me, urging me for more.

I thrust deeper and faster, taking my cues from her.

I want her to come first. I fucking need her to come first.

When she does, I follow right behind her with an intensity that burns through every part of me.

CHAPTER FORTY-TWO

Dylan

AN HOUR LATER, I'm on my couch in a pair of sweatpants while Eden sleeps in my bed.

I took her into the shower after we made love. I washed her under warm water as she hummed a song that we danced to the other night.

I stood and stared at her, basking in the rawness of her beauty, in the softness of her soul.

I've never met a better person than her.

She makes me want to be a better man.

I scoop the ring into my palm. I turn it to the left and then the right. The clear stones catch on the soft rays of light coming from the lamp in the corner.

Pride bubbled in my chest when I threw the winning touchdown during that game.

I looked over to see Coach on his feet, his hands in the air, and his beautiful daughter by his side.

She was only sixteen that day.

Too young for me to touch and too innocent to want to touch me.

She offered her palm in a high five when she hit the field in celebration with her dad. I curled my fingers around hers to savor the contact for just a few seconds.

Her eyes widened when I did it.

A flush of pink tainted the perfect skin of her cheeks. The color a match to the T-shirt she was wearing.

I knew that day that she had never been touched. I knew from the scowl on her dad's face when he caught me with her hand in mine, that I wouldn't be the guy who took her to bed for the first time.

He saw me as his son.

It was a line I couldn't cross. My respect for him back then trumped my need for her.

He's gone. She's here, and I need to level the playing field.

"Hey."

Her voice breaks through the memories. I turn to see her standing next to the couch. The band T-shirt covers her body.

I laugh. "I thought you hated that shirt."

She skims the bottom hem with her fingers. "On you, I do. I kind of like it on me."

"Keep it."

Her head shakes, sending her long hair skimming over her shoulders. "I'd rather keep the jersey. We can negotiate for it, can't we?"

I pat the couch next to me, wanting her beside me. "It's yours."

"Really?" She claps her hands together. "You don't want it?"

All I want is her forgiveness and a chance to spend every day I have left on this earth with her.

I take in a deep breath, warning myself to slow the hell down.

There are too many factors at play. I can't control it all, but I can control something.

She lowers herself to the couch, tucking one leg beneath her. I get a flash of the blue panties she was wearing earlier.

I could go at her again. I want to, but there's something I want to do more. There's something I need to do more.

'The ring." She looks down at my palm. "I remember the day you won it."

This is it. This is the moment when I take the opportunity she's unknowingly handing to me. I turn to face her, resting an arm over the back of the couch.

I stare at her face, knowing that she may never look at me like this again.

"Eden, I need to tell you something."

Her brows pinch at the stress woven into my tone. "What is it?"

I suck in a long breath, hoping that it will calm me. It doesn't work. "It's about the night we graduated."

Her expression lifts. "The night I found your ring."

The night I let you down.

The need to touch her is strong, but I resist. I want her to process this on her terms, in her way. She doesn't need to comfort me now. I'm the one who has to let her experience this and absorb it.

"You were never supposed to get in that car with Clark."

Her eyes search my face. "What do you mean?"

This may very well be the defining moment of my life.

Coach is dead. I could keep this buried for eternity. I can't be that man anymore.

Eden deserves better.

"Coach asked me to drive you home that night." I keep

my eyes pinned on her face. "I didn't follow through. I let you down. I let your dad down."

Time slows as she takes in each of my words. A string of emotions passes over her face. Surprise, then confusion. Finally, sadness settles there.

A tear wells in the corner of her eye. "You didn't let me down. You didn't let anyone down."

"I sure as hell did," I say without thinking, knowing that there's a lot more to this story to tell.

I can't spring it all on her at once. This is a starting point.

"Before I left for the party, my dad and I talked about how I would get home," she says softly. "He brought you up."

That's news to me. When Coach asked me earlier that day to drive Eden home, he told me to keep it under wraps. He didn't want her to think he was trying to control her every move.

"He was worried that Clark would drink too much beer." She sighs. "When he picked me up that night, he promised my dad he wouldn't drink. My dad told me I could go home with him as long as he didn't have a drop."

That explains why Clark had a bottle of water in his hand all night.

"You had to go to the airport." She tucks a strand of hair behind her ear. "Clark was sober. You didn't let me down, Dylan."

Relief should be washing over me, but there's another chapter to this story that needs to be told.

"Let's not talk about this now." Her lips find mine.

I kiss her softly. "Eden."

"Shh." Her fingers skim over my mouth. "Less talking. More kissing."

I nip at her fingers. "We can kiss later and talk more now."

She brushes a path over my eyebrow with her thumb. "I have to go soon. I need to catch a flight in the morning."

"Back to Buffalo?"

Her gaze drops. "Yes. Court at nine and then I'll stop by my office there."

Jealousy worms its way into my vision. I push it aside because I won't waste the time I have with her talking about another man.

My questions about Chet Richmond need to be put on ice for now.

"When will you be back in Manhattan?"

"Tomorrow night," she answers quickly. "I wouldn't miss our court date for anything."

That's going to happen the day after tomorrow. I need to see her again before we go head-to-head to fight over the remains of the Alcesters' shattered marriage.

"We'll meet for dinner."

I don't phrase it as a question because I don't want to give her the option of saying no.

"A drink?" she counters. "I have some prep I need to do before I beat you in court. I'll meet you at the Tin Anchor at eight. Do you know it?"

I represented the owner of the pub in a custody case.

"I'll be there at eight."

She plants one last, long, lingering kiss on my mouth. "I need to get dressed."

"I'll help," I offer, gliding a hand up her bare thigh.

"Why do I feel like you're offering to undress me instead?"

"Because I am."

CHAPTER FORTY-THREE

DYLAN

SEEING a familiar face is always a welcome sight.

I walk to the counter at Palla on Fifth and slap Kurt Sufford on the shoulder from behind.

"What the hell?" He turns to face me, his hand centered on his chest. "You scared me. Are you trying to give me a heart attack?"

I'd laugh under different circumstances, but I know he's been through a lot the last few weeks.

"It's good to see you, Kurt."

He edges his chin up. "Great to see you, Dylan. How's business?"

"Unhappiness never goes out of style." I point at the large herbal tea on the counter in front of him. "I see you're making some changes."

"This is the least of it." He runs a hand over his forehead. "Thelma has me up and out of bed at six every morning. First it's a walk in the park, oatmeal and fruit for breakfast once we're home."

"It's paying off." I cross my arms over my chest. "You're looking great."

He is. There's more color in his cheeks. His shoulders aren't tensed back. I've never seen him dressed in anything other than a tight three-piece suit. Today, he's wearing a pair of light brown dress pants and a white polo.

"I'm taking it day-by-day." He chuckles. "Change isn't easy. Backing off at work has been the hardest. So far I'm doing a lousy job. I'm keeping up with every case in both offices. Not an easy task when your wife wants you to do crossword puzzles and meditate."

I laugh. "You've got some good people running the ship while you rest up."

He takes a sip of the herbal tea. "You're talking about Eden. She's doing a great job here in Manhattan."

"And back in Buffalo," I point out. "I have to hand it to her. Two courtrooms in two different cities in two days. I don't know a lot of lawyers who could handle that and the flight in between."

His gaze narrows. "What the hell are you talking about?"

"Eden's in court in Buffalo today. We're facing off tomorrow in the Alcester case in front of Judge Mycella."

I doubt I'm giving away a secret. It has to be an oversight on his part. He's got over a hundred employees spread over two offices. Keeping track of all of them isn't an easy task.

He edges a finger over the bridge of his nose. "Eden's not in court today. She booked the day off."

That makes zero sense. She left my place last night in route to Noelle's so she could rest up before her early morning flight.

"You're sure?"

"One hundred percent sure." He taps his forehead. "Eden called me a couple of days ago to check-in. She mentioned needing a personal day today. I gave her my blessing because sometimes you need to rest before you face the lion."

I take it that I'm the lion in that analogy.

If she's not in court in Buffalo, where the hell is she?

He glances over my shoulder. "It's been good seeing you, Dylan. I need to run. I'm meeting with my partners. Retirement is on the horizon. I need to start thinking about who will fill my shoes."

Eden is the logical choice, so I point that out. "Eden must be at the top of the short list."

His mouth curves into a smile. "I agree, but she doesn't."

I query him with a raise of both brows.

He shrugs. "Off the record, I already offered her the job. She turned me down. No explanation. Nothing. Just 'thanks, but no thanks.'"

Something inside of me splinters. Maybe it's hope. I've rarely experienced it in my life, so I'm not an expert on what it feels to have your dreams torn in two.

She'd rather go back to Buffalo than stay in New York.

Just as Kurt's about to walk away, I stop him with another question. Curiosity fuels it because maybe he asked her before that first night at the club. Maybe he needs to pose the question to her again because circumstances have changed. Everything has changed in the past few weeks.

"When did you offer her the job?"

"During that call two days ago." He chuckles. "She said she'd think about it so I gave it one last valiant attempt last night in an email, but she replied before dawn today to let me off easy. It looks like Buffalo is where she wants to be."

———

"SHE'S NOT HERE, MR. COLT," Betsy Burton looks up at me. "She has the day off."

"It's my understanding that she's in Buffalo." I shoot her a dimpled smile. "Can you check to see if her court session is done for the day?"

"I have Ms. Conrad's Buffalo schedule right here." She taps a fingernail on her laptop screen. "There's nothing booked for her."

I'm not surprised. Kurt may be recovering from major heart surgery, but he's got a finger on the pulse of his employees.

He knows what they're up to.

I could wait for Eden to meet me for a drink tonight or I can push Betsy to get to the bottom of it.

I choose the latter because I've tried calling Eden and it went straight to voicemail. The two text messages I sent her asking about how her day is going have gone unanswered.

"Can I get the number of her assistant in Buffalo?" I lean on the reception desk with both forearms. "I need to get in touch with Eden regarding our court date tomorrow."

Her eyes widen. "Oh, that's right. The Alcesters go to court tomorrow."

I'm playing a hand I didn't intend, but I'll see it through to the end since Betsy is finally responding.

"Let me call her assistant myself." She points at the phone on her desk. "I'll explain the situation. She'll understand the urgency. The Alcester case is a priority, after all. Excuse me for a minute, will you?"

I step back to give her the privacy she needs to make the call.

It's not far enough that I can't hear her side of the conversation.

She greets someone on the other end of the call. That's

followed by a conversation about the weather in New York City. It's hot as hell here, and apparently that fascinates Betsy because she drags the discussion past the three-minute mark.

She finally gets down to the reason for her call.

I take a half-step closer so I don't miss a word.

"I see," she says. "Of course, Ms. Conrad needed to be there."

That's followed by a series of 'uh-huh's and 'oh, yeses'.

Frustration draws me even closer. Betsy doesn't notice me inching up on her because she's circling a pen on a piece of paper.

"I won't mention that to him," she half-whispers. "I won't say a thing about Eden's husband to Mr. Colt."

CHAPTER FORTY-FOUR

DYLAN

ANXIETY THREADS its way through every one of my movements.

It started when I shaved my face bare this morning.

I haven't done that in months.

It was a regular part of my routine for years, and this morning, in my dazed state, I reached for the razor. I came out of the shower and glanced at the mirror at a face I didn't recognize.

I walked right past Palla on Fifth on my way to my office.

Gunner was greeted with a wave of my hand.

He took it to heart, trailing after me like I had just granted his greatest wish.

I did when I turned at the doorway of my office to embrace him.

I needed the hug more than he did.

I'm skilled in handling difficult situations. Some of my

clients have told me that they've never met anyone as cold-hearted as me.

I've always taken it as a compliment.

I never will again.

Eden Conrad's ex-husband is the purest definition of a cold-hearted bastard.

He's rotting in prison just outside of Buffalo.

After the parole hearing she attended yesterday, he should be stuck there for at least the next two years.

"We need to get to the courthouse." Gunner appears in the doorway of my office. "I tried Ms. Conrad's cell again, sir, but it's going straight to voicemail."

I've tried it over and over again.

It started last night when she texted me to tell me that all flights out of Buffalo were grounded because of a band of thunderstorms that had rolled into the area.

I missed the text because I was in the middle of a dinner meeting with Trudy.

The text message I sent in reply was delivered but never read.

It was simple and to the point.

Dylan: I need you back here.

Worry settled over me when I woke at four thirty-five this morning and realized that she still hadn't read the message.

If she's in bed with Chet Richmond, I'll fight until my dying breath to make her see that I'm the better choice.

I am the better choice.

I have always been the better choice for her. I wish to fuck I would have acted on that before she got into that car with Clark Dodson, or married Dr. Aron Steiner.

"I'll call for an Uber." Gunner's gaze drops to his phone. "I got you a coffee from Palla on Fifth, sir. Is there anything else you need?"

Eden. I need Eden more than I need my next breath.

"Ms. Conrad will be at the courthouse," Gunner offers as if he's read my mind. "Let's head over there now."

He doesn't need to tag along, but I'm not going to protest.

I need the company.

Rising from my chair, I nod.

Gunner rushes toward me, his hands moving in the air in front of him. "Let me fix your tie, sir. It's crooked."

I let him have at it as I stare past him to the open door of my office.

"That's perfect." He pats my shoulder.

I follow him out of my office.

All I have to do is keep it together in court. After that, I can wrap the woman I love in my arms and never let her go.

———

SITTING NEXT to Trudy in the courtroom, I stare down at the watch on my wrist.

Eden has less than five minutes to get here.

The table where she should already be seated next to Troy is vacant.

"Maybe Troy has finally realized that he can't win this." Trudy laughs. "You're the big bad wolf. You scared them both away."

Her hand lands on my bicep. She squeezes it through my suit jacket.

I jerk my arm away. "What the hell, Trudy?"

Her eyes widen to saucers. She leans closer to me, dropping her voice to a whisper. "What? I know what you're about. I've seen you at Veil East enough times to know what you like."

Jesus.

"My friend, Corinne, told me all about you." She lets out a stuttered breath. "Why do you think I called you to represent me? I can't wait for us to celebrate the win."

I stare at her. "Nothing is going to happen between us whether we win this case or not."

"Says the lawyer who has screwed half of Manhattan." She shakes her head. "Corinne says the view from your penthouse is to die for, but the view under your suit is even better."

"I'm not saying that I haven't met fun guys at the club." She fans her hand in front of her face. "None of them measure up to you. If you know what I mean."

Regret pools in my gut.

Regret for all the years I've wasted with other women; years that I could have been building a life with Eden.

I glance to the left when Troy passes by.

I turn in my seat to catch a glimpse of Eden, but that's not who is trailing behind him.

Martin Durtow, a lawyer who works at Kurt's firm, tosses me a wave. "It's good to see you, Dylan."

I can't say the same.

Dread washes over me.

Something is wrong. Something is seriously fucking wrong.

I push to my feet and face him. "Where the hell is Eden?"

CHAPTER FORTY-FIVE

DYLAN

MARTIN POINTS at the bailiff as he enters the courtroom.

I remain standing, yanking my arm away when Trudy latches onto it as leverage to get herself out of the chair.

Tapping my shoe impatiently on the floor, I listen to the bailiff call court in session.

The Judge takes her seat, sips her water, runs a hand over her hair, and finally looks up.

Her brow pinches as she catches sight of Troy and his attorney.

"What's going on here?" Her finger points in their direction. "I wasn't informed of the change in counsel."

"I'm a last-second replacement, your honor," Martin says. "I haven't had time to get up to pace with the case. I'm requesting a short continuance."

"Is he serious?" Trudy grabs hold of my forearm. "I need this to be over, Dylan. Make it happen."

Turning to face Martin again, I repeat my question. "Where the hell is Eden?"

"Mr. Colt," Judge Mycella calls out. "Watch the language."

I glance at her briefly before I level my gaze on Martin. "Where is Eden?"

"This is my courtroom, Mr. Colt." Judge Mycella reminds me with a sharp note in her tone. "I'll ask the questions."

I open my mouth to repeat my question, but she continues, "Mr. Durtow, are you replacing Ms. Conrad as counsel for Mr. Alcester?"

A sudden burst of applause escapes from the gallery.

I feel like I'm in the middle of a goddamn circus.

The judge bangs her gavel once. "Order in the court."

I take a step closer to Martin. "I need to know where Eden Conrad is."

"Mr. Colt." The Judge shoots me a look that is meant to shut me the hell up. "One more outburst and you'll be found in contempt."

"Ms. Conrad is unavailable," Martin says in an even tone.

Judge Mycella nods. "Very well."

No. Not very well. No fucking way.

"I need a sidebar, your honor." I start walking toward her. "Now."

Her brow twists in confusion. "Alright. Fine. Counsel will approach."

Martin takes his sweet time walking to the bench. "What's the issue here, Dylan?"

"My question as well," Peggy says, glaring at me.

I fist my hands at my sides. "I need you to tell me where Eden Conrad is."

"I don't see how that's your business." Martin tucks his hands in the pockets of his pants.

I shoot Peggy a look. "It's my business."

"Mr. Colt and Ms. Conrad are old friends," Peggy explains. "I think it's safe to say that Mr. Colt is surprised by the change in counsel and his question is related to concern for his friend."

"Exactly." I tap a hand on the bench to avoid wrapping it around Martin's neck.

I want a fucking answer to my question.

Martin scrubs his forehead with his hand. "In that case, I suppose it's fine to tell you."

I wait while he gazes down at the floor before he finally looks at me.

"Eden was on her way back from Buffalo early this morning." He leans closer, lowering his voice. "She was driving. There was an accident."

I reach for the bench to steady myself.

Christ. No. Please no.

Peggy gasps. "Oh, my goodness. What is her condition?"

"Where is she?" I blurt out. "Tell me where she is?"

"I don't know her condition." He lowers his voice. "All I know is that she was in a car wreck."

"A continuance." I thump my fisted hand on the bench. "I need a continuance."

"Granted." Peggy doesn't miss a beat as she brings the gavel down. "We're adjourned until a week from now."

————

BEFORE WE HIT THE ELEVATOR, Gunner is on the phone with Lennox Hill Hospital. I'm waiting for Betsy Burton to pick up.

I cut her off before she can finish her greeting. "Betsy,

this is Dylan Colt. I need to know everything you know about Eden Conrad."

Gunner and I stand steady when the elevator doors fly open. Cell service is shit in there. I have someone on the line that can tell me about Eden, so I'm not moving a muscle.

"I'm not at liberty to share personal information about our employees," Betsy says with a tremor in her voice.

"Bullshit," I spit back. "I need you to tell me now where I can find Eden."

Jesus, please let her be all right. Don't let this be the end.

"Mr. Sufford has made it very clear that we cannot give…"

I end the call, cursing under my breath at the woman's commitment to following the rules.

I open my contact list and scroll down to Kurt's name.

I look over at Gunner while I wait for Kurt to pick up.

He's spelling Eden's name out to someone at New York Presbyterian.

My call to Kurt rings through to voicemail. I spit out a few words. "It's Dylan Colt. I need to know where Eden is. Call me back as soon as you can."

Ending the call, I turn to Gunner. "Get me Noelle Sufford's number."

We board the elevator headed to the ground floor. I have no idea which direction I'm supposed to go when I get off this thing, but I'll find her.

If she's taken her last breath, I would feel it inside.

Eden is alive, and I'm going to get to her.

CHAPTER FORTY-SIX

DYLAN

ONE BENEFIT of being a divorce lawyer for the wealthy and elite in Manhattan is that a stack of favors is at your disposable.

I cashed in today.

Noelle Sufford was at LaGuardia when Gunner reached her.

I didn't ask how he managed to track down her cell number. I don't care.

He came through when I needed it.

He backed that up with a call to a former client who offered the use of his private plane.

Noelle hitched a ride with me.

She didn't say much on the flight. I was fine with that. My focus is only on Eden.

Seeing her, helping her, loving her.

We touched down in Buffalo twenty minutes ago. We're walking through the main doors of the General Hospital now.

I don't have to ask Noelle if she's been here before. It's obvious she has.

She leads me down a series of corridors until we're standing next to a reception desk in the emergency room.

"Good day." The woman behind the desk has a tone to cheery for the job. "What can I do for you two?"

"I'm Dr. Noelle Sufford." Noelle rakes a hand through her hair. "I'm here to see a patient. Eden Conrad."

The woman taps on a keyboard in front of her. She pecks away with one finger. "Yes. Ms. Conrad is here."

"Where?" I blurt out.

The woman behind the desk looks up at me. "She's under the care of one of our physicians. If you have a seat, I'll have the doctor come speak to you."

"What's the attending physician's name?" Noelle looks down a long corridor. People dressed in green scrubs and white lab coats are darting in and out of doorways.

"Dr. Joy Yelena."

Noelle points at a phone on the woman's desk. "Please let her know that Dr. Noelle Sufford is here waiting to speak to her."

The woman gives her a nod.

"Do you know Eden's doctor?" I ask, hoping that Noelle has enough influence to get us in front of Eden as soon as possible.

She offers me a small smile. "We've met. Let's sit and wait."

I follow her to a row of plastic chairs and take a seat next to her. "She needs to be okay."

Noelle's hand lands on my shoulder. "She's the strongest person I've ever known. I have faith that she'll come through this."

She has to. I can't live the rest of my life without her.

————

DR. YELENA'S gaze is trained on Noelle's face.

She's explaining Eden's condition to her in terms I don't understand.

I listen intently, tuned in to words I recognize.

They are few and far between.

Tired of waiting for their discussion to end, I interrupt. "Is Eden going to be all right? Can I see her?"

Dr. Yelena looks directly at me for the first time. "Who are you?"

Noelle stutters out a non-answer. "Eden and…they went to high school…but they have something now…I don't know how…"

I let out a deep breath. "I love her."

Noelle gasps. "You love her?"

I look over at her. "Deeply."

Her eyes widen. "Does she know that?"

"She will." I turn my attention back to the doctor. "As soon as I'm allowed in to see her, she'll know how much I love her."

Dr. Yelena nods. "I'll make that happen as soon as I can. We're running tests. Give me some time."

"Is she conscious?" Noelle asks, her voice wavering.

"She is." Dr. Yelena steals a glance over her shoulder to the corridor. "I need to get back to her. I can tell you that she's awake. She's disoriented and in pain. When I have an update, I'll be back."

I turn to Noelle when the doctor walks away. "Is she going to be all right?"

Tears well in the corners of her eyes. "She'll be okay. She's going to come through this."

Relief hits me with the full force of a tidal wave. I drop back in the chair, cover my face with my hands, and exhale.

I won't waste this chance. I fucking won't let her get away again.

Eden Conrad is everything to me, and the moment I'm in front of her, she'll know that.

CHAPTER FORTY-SEVEN

DYLAN

EDEN LOOKS SO small and fragile in the hospital bed.

Her bottom lip is twice the size it normally is. The area around her right eye is swollen and shaded purple and yellow.

Her left arm is in a sling.

She's beautiful.

She's the only woman I've ever loved.

"Try not to wake her." Dr. Yelena raises a finger to her lips. "You're both welcome to stay, but I'd advise you to get some rest. She'll be here for the night. We will reevaluate in the morning."

She steps out of the room, leaving Noelle and me with a nurse.

The gray-haired woman pushes a black tote bag at Noelle. "This was brought in with her."

Noelle reaches for it. "I'll take care of it."

"This is the content of her pockets." The nurse passes a

small, clear plastic bag to Noelle. "I'll be right outside if you need anything."

"I think I'll go to her place and get some rest." Noelle fishes her hand in the tote bag. "Her condo keys must be in here."

I can't take my eyes off of Eden.

I have no intention of going anywhere.

Griffin is covering for me until I'm back in New York.

Gunner is his back up. I spoke to him ten minutes ago with an update.

Noelle did the same with her dad. I heard her tell him that she'll be back in Manhattan tomorrow.

"I can't believe she still has this," Noelle whispers. "It's beautiful."

Whatever it is, it can't compare to Eden.

The soft jingle of keys fills the air, but Eden doesn't stir. The monitors hooked up to her beat on in a comforting rhythm.

"Will you text me if there's any change?" Noelle takes a step closer to me. "Her condo isn't far. I can be back here in a flash."

I glance over at her. "I'll text you if there's a change."

"Her dad died in a room two floors up." Her gaze drops. "She held onto this. She told me it gave her strength to get through it."

I look down at the piece of blue sea glass in her palm.

"Give it to her if she wakes up." She pushes it into my hand. "It must still give her strength now. It was in the pocket of her pants tonight."

I curl my fist around it. "I'll see to it that she gets it."

"She hasn't had it easy." She tilts her head. "She deserves to be happy."

"I'll do everything in my power to make that happen."

She glances over at Eden. "I can tell that you will."

———

I ROLL the piece of sea glass in my hand.

It's been hours since Noelle left.

Eden hasn't moved. Her breathing is still calm. Her lip is more swollen than it was earlier.

"I love you," I whisper. "I wanted to tell you the night we graduated."

I take her right hand, cupping it in mine.

"I'm sorry that I let you down." I choke back a sob. "I'm so sorry that I hurt you."

I rest my lips against her open palm. A smudge of dried blood is there.

I reach for a tissue to rub it off, trying to ward off the mental image of the accident.

The nurse who is watching over Eden had only sparse details to share. She got those from the paramedics who were on scene.

The roads were wet and slick. Eden's car careened down an embankment and came to rest against a tree.

The airbag deployed.

That likely saved her life.

"I should have been there to protect you from all of it." I press her hand to my cheek. "From everything you've been through."

One of her fingers brushes against the side of my nose.

My eyes pop open. "Eden? Wake up."

Her fingers stir again, branching out across my cheek.

"It's me," I whisper against her cheek. "Open your beautiful eyes."

She does.

Slow flutters of her eyelashes reveal those gorgeous blue irises.

"Eden," I choke back a sob. "I'm here."

She swallows, wincing in pain.

"I'll get the doctor." I start to pull away. "Let me get the nurse."

"Dylan," she whispers my name so softly that I can barely make it out over the beeping of the monitor. "Am I dreaming?"

I huff out a laugh. "You're awake. Thank fuck you're awake."

Squinting, she studies my face. "Are you eighteen-year-old Dylan? You look just like him."

I rub a hand over my jaw and the light five o'clock shadow that's settled there. "You like him."

Her grip on my face tightens. "Kiss me."

I do it. Softly and tenderly, being mindful of the crack on her swollen lip.

Her eyes find mine. Panic washes over her expression. "Is he okay?"

From my understanding, she was alone in her car, and it was a single vehicle accident.

"Who?"

Her gaze searches my face. "There was a deer on the road. I tried so hard not to hit it. Please tell me he's okay."

I have no idea if the deer survived, so I offer what I can. "I'm going to get the doctor. She'll come check on you, and I'll check on the deer."

She swallows again. "You'll come right back?"

I slide the piece of sea glass from my hand into hers. "I'm not going anywhere."

Her fingers play over the smooth surface. A tear slides down her cheek. "Do you promise?"

I chase the tear away with a brush of my thumb over her skin. "I promise."

CHAPTER FORTY-EIGHT

Eden

DYLAN and I haven't been alone since last night.

After I woke up, two doctors rushed in. They ran me through a battery of tests, asking if I knew my name, and where it hurts.

It hurts everywhere.

I drifted back to sleep after that, and when I woke up this morning, Noelle was by my side.

Dylan was still in the room, standing at the foot of the hospital bed with his hands in the pockets of his pants.

The pieces of what happened are starting to fall into place.

After all the flights to New York City were canceled because of the bad weather, I decided to drive so I'd make it to court in time.

I packed a few things into my car and set off.

The next thing I remember is a deer on the road, and then waking up here.

The doctor told me that a state trooper found me and that the deer must have ran off. I have no idea how long I was unconscious.

"I'm going back to Manhattan." Noelle moves to give me a side hug being mindful of the sling on my left arm. "It's best if you don't travel for a couple of days. Promise me that you'll go back and see Dr. Yelena tomorrow."

I nod. "I promise."

Dylan's been almost silent since we got to my condo. He held my hand in the Uber on the way here. He carried me up the stairs against my protests.

I didn't have to ask him to stay in Buffalo with me.

He bought a few changes of clothes and a new charger for his phone.

"I don't want to miss my flight." Noelle glides a hand over my forehead. "If you need anything, you'll call me?"

I glance over to where Dylan is standing. "I have everything I'll ever need."

———

I KICK OFF MY BOOTS, sending one flying onto a leather chair in the corner.

"Your aim is remarkable." Dylan laughs. "What can I do for you?"

I move to stand next to the window. My condo doesn't offer a view of anything other than the parking lot.

I stare out at the blue sky beyond.

I sense Dylan behind me before his hand brushes over my bare shoulder. I'm wearing an oversized blue sweater and a pair of leggings. Noelle chose them for ease and comfort.

"Can I get you some water or maybe something to eat?"

He nestles his chin against the top of my head. "A full body massage perhaps?"

I rest my back against his broad chest. "Do you know?"

I feel the nod of his head before he says anything. "I know that I can't live without you."

I turn to face him. It's there in the way he's been looking at me and in the kiss of his lips last night and this morning.

I repeat the words back because I've never spoken anything that feels so right. "I can't live without you."

His fingers rest on my chin. Tilting my head up so our eyes meet, he smiles. "I love you, Eden."

It feels as though I've been waiting my entire life for those four words to leave his lips. "I love you too."

He presses his mouth to mine.

"I need to tell you things." I look over at two cardboard boxes near the front door. "I have a lot to tell you."

His gaze settles on my lips. "Dr. Yelena made it clear that you need to rest. Let's do that together. You can close your eyes for an hour, two tops. Once you've done that, we can talk."

I do feel dizzy, and the doctor was adamant that I need rest.

"You'll wake me after an hour?" I ask.

"We can negotiate that," he says with a chuckle. "With the understanding that all agreed to terms will be set back until a date when you're up for the action."

"I want to make love," I say it because I need him to know.

I'm in pain. I'm still reeling from the past twenty-four hours, but I've never wanted him more.

"We have all the time in the world for that." He kisses my forehead. "Let's get you into bed. Sleep now. Talk later."

I don't argue as he leads me down the hallway to my bedroom.

I'm going to fall asleep in my bed wrapped in Dylan's arms. Another of my dreams is about to come true.

CHAPTER FORTY-NINE

Dylan

I SHOOT off a text to Barrett to let him know that Eden is on the mend.

He offered to make the trip here to lend a hand, but I assured him that I had everything covered.

I do.

Early this morning, while Eden was still fast asleep in her hospital bed and Noelle was by her side, I came to her condo.

I bought groceries, fresh coffee beans, and a bouquet of roses for the woman I love.

I wanted her to have everything she could ever possibly need.

I needed the same for myself, so I called Tony Girano and put him to work.

He was already digging into Eden's ex-husband's life for me. He unearthed a treasure trove of unsealed court records.

Aron Steiner stalked Eden when she broke free of him. He was arrested for that, but his evil had no bounds.

He threatened his second wife. He terrorized her with harassing phone calls and in-person visits despite a restraining order.

Her constant refusal to engage in a discussion with him sent him over the edge.

He assaulted a colleague of his.

Eden made the trip to Buffalo to speak at his parole hearing. It's the second time she's done that.

I glance down at the screen of my phone when another email from Tony comes through.

I click to open the attachment.

Disbelief clouds my vision. I blink a few times to focus.

It's a death certificate.

Clark Dodson died seven years ago in Virginia. Cardiac arrest is listed as the manner of death.

He didn't make it out of his twenties.

"Dylan?" Eden calls from the bedroom. "Are you here?"

"I'm here," I say, pushing to my feet from the chair I settled in near her living room window. "I'll always be here."

———

I CLEAR the plates after we both finish eating our dinner.

"Those pancakes were better than the place in New York." Eden leans back on the soft leather couch. "You're a great cook."

I walk back into the living room. "Anyone can make pancakes."

I take a seat beside her again.

Confessions cleanse the soul, but they can unleash destruction.

I can move forward with this woman with my secret

intact. The only other person who knows what I did on the night of our graduation is dead.

Eden would never know, but I will always know that I've kept something from her.

"You know I was married, don't you?" She tugs on the shoulder of the sweater she's wearing. "I want to explain that."

She doesn't need to.

I understand. The pull toward him must have been strong for her to take that step.

I won't let her share her secrets until I share mine.

"You're away from him and safe. That's what matters." I rest a hand on her knee. "I need to tell you something."

"Have you been married?" Her voice cracks. "You've been married, haven't you?"

I chuckle. "Fuck no."

She lets out a breathy sigh. "Why am I so happy about that?"

I want that smile on her face to last. I want her to wake up every day for the rest of her life and look at me with that much joy.

I owe her this. I owe us this.

If we start with a clean slate, the world is no match for us.

"Something happened on graduation night."

Her eyes skim my face. "I know. You left. I was in an accident. It's history."

I take a deep, steadying breath. "Something else happened."

Anger took hold of Clark when I walked out of that bedroom and faced him. I did something that a jealous, petty eighteen-year-old kid would do when the girl he liked picked another guy to love.

I wanted him to dump her.

I needed him to send her packing so she'd give up on Ohio State and make a life in New York City without her dad watching over her.

"What else happened?"

I move to sit on the coffee table so that I can face her directly. I want her to look into my eyes when I tell her this. I need her to understand the depth of my regret.

What is it, Dylan?" Her hand reaches for mine.

I take it and squeeze it, needing the comfort only her touch can provide. "I said something to Clark before I left that party."

Her eyes widen. "What did you say?"

Something that set him off to the point that he pushed me. I slammed him back against the wall with a veiled threat that I'd end his football career with a snap of his tattooed arm.

I was taller than him. I weighed a good twenty pounds more.

He backed down. Brushing past me he went into the bedroom I had just exited.

The same bedroom that I'd left Eden in.

I take a deep breath. "I made him believe that something had happened between us in that bedroom."

Her gaze drops to her lap.

"You told me you were going to Ohio State. I stormed out of the room."

"I remember," she says quietly.

"I had a pair of panties in my pocket," I go on, "a girl had shoved them at me when I got to the party. I tugged them out so Clark would think…"

"That we made love in that bedroom?" Her eyes meet mine.

That was my intention. I wanted him to think that I had

taken what he wanted most in the world. I needed him to believe that I'd claimed her virginity.

He did believe it. He shot words at me about his property and my filthy dick being near her.

I left her in a room with his anger and then she got in a car with him.

Sorry is inadequate, so I fumble for the right words. "I was wrong. It was a stupid thing to do."

Tears wash over her eyes.

I bring her hand to my mouth. "I'm so sorry."

"We didn't crash because of what you said to him, Dylan." She looks into my eyes. "You had nothing to do with what happened to us that night."

CHAPTER FIFTY

Eden

CLARK DODSON WAS the boy I thought I would eventually love.

I think that was because my dad loved the promise that he held and I wanted to give my dad the world after everything he had done for me.

Clark had a throwing arm that brought scouts from some of the nation's best football schools to his games.

He was edgy and good-looking.

Tattoos covered his body. His dark hair was always a spikey mess.

He smoked clove cigarettes and got good grades.

My dad told me that Clark would take 'us' to the NFL.

Clark's prospects were good. He was offered a full ride athletic scholarship to Ohio State, but everything changed on the night we graduated.

We left the graduation party together.

Our relationship was mostly handholding and a few stolen kisses.

Clark would sometimes talk about marrying me.

For a girl who believed in romantic fairytales, it should have been exciting.

I had visions of a career on Broadway, a husband who loved me, and at least two children.

The only problem was that the face of the husband in my dreams didn't belong to Clark. It belonged to Dylan.

"When Clark came into the bedroom, he asked me if we had kissed."

Dylan's expression shifts. "Kissed? He didn't ask if we fucked?"

I shake my head. I remember everything about that night. "No. He asked if we had kissed. I laughed and told him that we talked."

"What happened then?"

"He laughed too." I close my eyes briefly, a rush of memories flooding me all at once. "He kissed me. He told me he was tired. I told him we could leave."

"He trusted you," he says quietly. "He didn't believe me."

He's right. Clark trusted me just as much as I trusted him. I was holding a secret for him that he knew I'd never share.

It was sacred to him.

"We had a bond," I explain. "He needed someone in his corner who would never betray him. That's who I was to him."

Dylan nods.

"I didn't love him," I clarify. "I don't think he ever loved me, but I knew something about him that connected us."

"What do you mean?" Curiosity knits Dylan's brow.

"Clark had a secret," I admit softly. "Only his dad and I knew."

My relationship with Clark fell apart the night of the accident. The secret his father had tried so hard to keep buried was unearthed.

I saw him only a handful of times after the accident.

He begged for my forgiveness. I begged him to take care of himself.

He didn't. He died a few years later without getting the surgery that may have saved his life.

I look up for forgiveness even though I know Clark would grant it unconditionally.

"What was the secret?" Dylan asks gently.

"Clark had a heart condition." I circle my thumb over Dylan's hand. "It was serious enough that he shouldn't have been playing football."

"I had no idea."

"I promised I'd never tell anyone." I hang my head. "He told me one night because he couldn't keep it in. He was scared. I told him I'd always be there for him. He needed me to always be there for him."

Dylan's eyes search my face.

"He fainted behind the wheel the night of the accident." I close my eyes. "I reached over to take control of the car, but it was too late."

Taking my face in his hands, Dylan kisses my cheek. "I had no idea that's what happened that night."

"No one did," I whisper. "After the accident, everyone did. It ended his football career. It ended everything."

———

I SIP water from the glass that Dylan handed me.

It pains me to know that he's lived with guilt for so long. I had no idea that he had tried to trick Clark into believing that we had made love in a stranger's bedroom in a house I'd never been to.

Clark would have been angry with Dylan for saying something like that about me, but he would never have believed it.

My virginity was important to me.

Clark respected that.

I did until the accident.

The pain of it and the long road to recovery changed me. I sought out short- term connections to feed a need inside of me.

One of those short-term connections was with Dr. Aron Steiner.

He was ten years old than me, very successful, and handsome.

His need to control me broke us apart, but it didn't stop his obsession.

"You and Clark were over after the accident?" Dylan asks gently. "You didn't leave Chicago that summer?"

I shake my head. "No. I stayed there until we moved to Boston for school."

"We?"

"My dad went with me." I smile. "He got a job at a high school there coaching ball. He loved it."

The corners of Dylan's lips curve up. "Football was his life."

It was. My dad lived and breathed the game. If he wasn't on a field, he was watching a game on TV.

"Did he follow you to Buffalo after you passed the bar?"

I'm quiet for a second. "After I got married, my dad moved to Buffalo. Kurt used his connections to land my dad a coaching job at a high school there."

"You and your ex settled there after you were done school?" His brows perk.

I know it can't be easy for him to mention my ex-husband, but he's part of my past.

I've tried to forget about Aron, but I can't.

I'll do whatever I can to keep him behind bars for as long as I can.

"I took a job in Monroe County." I don't bother adding that Aron opened an office there as a General Practitioner once I was settled into my job.

"What am I missing?" He narrows his eyes. "Kurt's practice was in full swing by then. You could have handled divorces in the big city instead of in a small county, and you would have been closer to your dad. Did your ex-husband have work there?"

I swallow. "I wasn't handling divorces. I was a prosecutor."

CHAPTER FIFTY-ONE

EDEN

I GLANCE over at the cardboard boxes next to my front door.

One has bedroom scrawled across the side. The other is labeled kitchen items. I packed them before I got in my car to drive to Manhattan.

"You were a prosecutor?" Dylan punctuates the words with an arch of his right eyebrow. "What was that like?"

Stressful. Difficult. Exhilarating. Fulfilling.

"I loved it," I admit. "I was excited to go to my office every day."

"Why did you make the switch from that to working for Kurt?"

I skim my fingertip over my top lip. I answer in the simplest terms. "Money."

Aron and I split with an agreement in place that we'd both walk away with what we brought to the marriage. I fought hard for that. I didn't want to accept anything from a man I no longer had an ounce of respect for.

With that came a feeling of freedom and independence. I've never regretted the decision to turn down the large settlement he offered me.

I never wanted to be in his debt in any way.

My decision was right for me, even months later when my dad was diagnosed with lung cancer, and I faced the first of many medical bills.

Kurt saw that I was drowning so he made me an offer I couldn't refuse.

I packed my things, moved to Buffalo, and took care of my dad and his financial needs.

Carrying that burden for him was the right thing to do.

The move also gave me more time with him before he died.

Dylan's phone vibrates on the coffee table. He glances down at it. "It's Griffin calling."

"Take it," I suggest, needing a break from our conversation.

We've covered a lot of ground quickly.

It's good but exhausting and since I have more to tell, I need a break to recharge. "I'm going to take another nap."

"I'll come to tuck you in as soon as I'm done." He scoops his phone into his palm. "I'll be right there."

I let him help me up from the couch, waiting as he presses a kiss to my cheek. "I love you, Eden. I'll always love you."

"I love you too."

I always have.

———

I WAKE to a rush of desire when I feel Dylan's body wrap around mine from behind.

He's nude.

I am too.

He helped me undress, taking special care with the sling on my arm. I only suffered a sprain and not a fracture, which means I'll be healed in no time.

I invited him to join me under the covers, but he insisted that I sleep first.

When his lips brush over my bare shoulder, I'm grateful that he didn't let me sleep the entire night away.

"I called Dr. Yelena," he admits on a sigh.

Worry crowds my thoughts. After the accident when I was seventeen, the doctor didn't tell me everything. He held things back because my dad asked him to.

It wasn't until the third surgery on my right leg that I realized that I'd never dance professionally.

I still suffer from pain in my legs, but it's not enough to steal away my love of dance for good.

I glance over my shoulder at his face. "Why?"

His features look softer in the darkened room. "I wanted to be sure it was safe."

"You wanted to be sure what was safe?"

I'm not sure if it's the minor concussion I suffered or sleepiness, but I finally realize what he's talking about as the question leaves my mouth.

"Oh, you're talking about…"

His hand skims over my hip. "I know you're tender. She said I had to be gentle, so we're not going all out tonight, but I want to do one thing for you."

I close my eyes, relishing in the way his fingers are gliding over my hipbone. "What do you want to do for me?"

His hand moves slowly, trailing a path over my stomach until it dives lower. "I want to touch you, kiss you. I want to feel you come."

I roll onto my back, wincing from the pain in my shoulder. "I want those things too."

He brushes his soft lips over my collarbone. "You don't have to move a muscle. Let me help you feel."

I breathe out on a heavy exhale when he slides down my body, nestling his shoulders between my legs.

He parts me with his fingers. That lightest touch ignites something deep inside of me. I moan. "Dylan, please."

"You're so fucking beautiful." His tongue skims my cleft. "I love you so much."

"I love you," I whisper in a breathy moan.

I tangle my fingers in his hair as he takes me with his mouth.

CHAPTER FIFTY-TWO

DYLAN

"DYLAN COLT." I hold out a hand to the man because I'm a decent human being, and I can't exactly tell him to go straight to hell with Eden and another woman looking on.

"Hey, buddy." Chet Richmond ignores my hand and goes all in for a full-on hug.

I let him take it where he needs to because Eden is beaming like sunshine.

The guy has some strength in his arms. When he finally lets me go, he gives me a quick pat on the cheek with his palm.

I swear to fuck it's almost as hard as a slap. I consider lifting my hand to his face to return the favor, but I step back and wrap my arm around Eden's shoulder.

She's mine, dude. Back the hell off.

That's the intended meaning of my actions.

I think the message got lost somewhere because Chet does the same with the tall blonde he's standing next to.

"We're getting married," he declares.

I look down at Eden because her reaction is all I care about.

The smile on her face says it all. She's happy. She's genuinely happy that her on and off again boyfriend is taking the plunge with someone else.

"I didn't even know you two were dating." She leans forward to check out the diamond on the blonde woman's hand.

No one has bothered to introduce us yet, so I take that small matter into my hands.

"Congratulations." I offer her the same hand I offered her fiancé, but I take a step back so there's no chance she'll rush in for a hug. "We haven't been introduced yet. I'm Dylan."

"June Bug," she says.

I furrow my brow because I have no idea if that's her actual name or a nickname. Eden doesn't flinch, and Chet's about to shed a tear, so I go with it.

"It's good to meet you, June."

"Bug," she adds.

"June works with us." Eden looks up at me. "She started in the office about three months ago, I think."

"Three-and-a-half," June corrects her. "It was love at first sight."

"Instantaneous," Chet chimes in. "I knew it when I first saw her. She's my forever."

"When is the wedding?" Eden bounces on her heels.

"Soon." June smiles. "You'll come back for it, won't you?"

Eden's gaze meets mine. "We'll come back for it, won't we, Dylan?"

I nod because I'll go anywhere with her.

It's the reason I followed her out of the bedroom when the

doorbell rang. I joked that the doorman would get it. Eden scoffed and told me that I was spoiled rotten.

We had both just finished getting dressed. It's barely nine a.m., but Eden didn't mind the intrusion. She invited Chet and June in as soon as she swung open the door to her condo.

"We want you to rest." Chet reaches for Eden's hand. "I was worried, Ed. I told everyone at work that you were too tough to let an accident keep you down for long."

Eden squeezes his hand briefly. "I'm glad you both stopped by."

"We ordered some flowers." June wraps a hand around Chet's bicep. "They'll be delivered this afternoon. If you need anything, you'll call us?"

Eden slides her hand into mine. "I have everything I need right here."

———

"I CAN BRUSH your hair if you want," I offer once Chet and June Bug take off.

Eden runs her right hand through her hair. "Why? Is it messy?"

Beautifully so.

"It's perfect." I sigh. "You're perfect."

She looks down at the simple light blue sundress I helped her get into earlier. I slid on her lingerie first, taking special care with her sprained arm. I adjusted the sling so there wasn't too much pressure on her neck.

I put on a new pair of jeans and a plain black T-shirt I bought yesterday.

"You can ask me the question," she says matter-of-factly.

"I don't have a ring yet," I say with a smirk.

A blush creeps high on her cheeks. "Oh, no. Gosh, no. I didn't mean that."

"You don't want to marry me?" I tease because I know damn well that if I dropped to a knee right now, she'd say yes.

I have the perfect ring in mind. I doubt it exists, so when I'm back in Manhattan, I'm going to visit Ivy Marlow-Walker. She's the owner of Whispers of Grace. She helped me design a necklace for my mom's birthday two years ago. I trust her with the task of bringing my vision of an engagement ring to life.

A brilliant sapphire will take center stage. Small diamonds will line the band.

I've given this some serious thought.

"You know the answer to that question." She glances down. "Don't ask me until the time is right."

"That's a deal," I agree with a nod of my head.

"I was talking about the question about what June meant when she asked if I'd be back for their wedding."

I'm a reasonably smart guy.

I noticed the cardboard boxes near the front door. I saw the business card of a Buffalo based real estate agent sitting on her kitchen counter.

I didn't give a lot of thought to the missed call on her phone yesterday from a guy named Darrell Carver.

I looked him up early this morning.

He's an Assistant District Attorney in Manhattan.

Eden's going back to her roots.

"I emailed June yesterday to ask her if she would be willing to take over two of my open cases here." She smiles. "I told her I needed time to recover from the accident, but it's more than that and I want you to be the first to know."

I don't interrupt because I want to hear the words from her.

"I'm going to accept a job at the prosecutor's office in New York. They offered me the position right before I came back here." Her gaze drops. "I'm not good at this divorce thing. I'm really good at putting bad guys away and keeping them there."

"You'll move in with me." I tuck a strand of hair behind her ear. "If you hate the place, we'll find a new apartment."

"I love your place." She smiles. "I didn't want to assume that we'd live together, but I have started packing."

"I'll finish that up." I flex my arms. "We'll get you moved in as soon as possible."

"I have work here that I need to see through to its end, and there's the Alcester case."

I tilt her chin up with my hand. "Griffin talked to Trudy. She's willing to agree to your most recent offer."

"You're not serious?" Her eyes light up. "Dylan, are you serious?"

Griffin told me that Eden's accident hit a chord with Trudy. Her dad had been in a car wreck when she was a kid, and she lost time with him during the recovery. It made her realize that shutting Troy out of their daughters' lives isn't the right thing to do.

"Griffin and Martin will close the case out." I breathe a sigh of relief. "It's over."

EPILOGUE

3 Months Later

EDEN

"I'M open to all offers, Mr. Colt." I hold up two bras. "If you want me to wear the red one tonight that will cost you a quickie in the shower, and if you…"

"A quickie?" Dylan snatches the red bra out of my hand. "Quickies are never part of our negotiations. I take my time with my beautiful fiancée. You should know that by now."

I glance up at my left hand and the beautiful sapphire engagement ring Dylan gave me last week.

It's been twelve weeks since my accident.

I'm fully healed.

We went out to celebrate that fact.

The night started with pancakes for dinner and ended with Dylan on one knee inside the club that Billy owns.

It was perfect and breathtaking and everything I could

have ever wished for.

After we danced, we came back to our apartment and made love.

"What will it cost me if I want you to wear the black one?" He eyes the black lace bra in my right hand.

"What are you offering?"

He slides the boxer briefs he's wearing down to mid-thigh.

His hand wraps around the root of his erection. "This."

"In my mouth?" I whisper.

"Wherever the fuck you want it?"

I toss the bra over my head. It lands somewhere on the bed.

I edge my legs apart just enough that I can slide a hand over my core. "I think I want it right here."

I gasp when he lunges at me.

He spins me around, dropping me onto my back on the bed.

His boxer briefs hit the floor in an instant.

He slides his big body over me. "Do you know how much I love you?"

I'll never tire of hearing it from him. He tells me as often as he can. He whispers it in my ear just as I'm falling asleep at night. It's the first thing I hear every morning.

I'm greeted with voicemail messages at work from Dylan telling me how the world brightened when I danced back into his life.

"Tell me." I inch my hips up so I can feel his cock pressing into my core.

He slides the tip into me. It's exquisite. The feeling of him bare when he enters me pulls a moan from my lips.

"I love you more than I thought it was possible," he whispers against my lips.

Plunging himself deeper, I gasp. "Dylan."

"I love you for every beautiful memory you've given me and all the promise that is ahead of us."

I close my eyes because it's so much. It's all-consuming.

He thrusts over and over, pushing me closer to the edge.

"You, my beautiful Eden, are what my every dream is made of."

I dig my fingernails into the skin of his shoulder. "I love you."

"Forever." He pumps harder and faster.

"Forever," I repeat back, biting his lip.

Pleasure pulses through me as he works his cock in long strokes.

I cry out when the orgasm hits me. I cling to him, twisting beneath him as he fucks me through one climax and straight into another.

————

"I CHANGED the locks today so Gunner can't just show up whenever the hell he wants." Dylan comes strolling into our living room dressed in a tailored black suit, a black shirt, and a blue tie.

He's gorgeous.

I twirl in place. The black dress I'm wearing lifts up to reveal my thighs.

I was wearing this dress when we first saw each other at the club.

"Gunner loves you," I pout. "That makes me kind of love him."

Adjusting one of his cuff links, Dylan lets out a hearty laugh. "He keeps telling me that he's great with kids. I keep telling him that we're giving it a couple of years."

It's what we both want.

We'll get married at the end of the year.

We need time to love each other before we add a baby to our world and I need time to settle into my new job as an assistant district attorney.

Adding to our family will happen when the time is right.

Dylan is determined to cut his workload once we do become parents.

"Are you ready?" Dylan gives me the once-over. "Because you look like a million bucks, Ms. Conrad."

"I could say the same for you." I smile. "We didn't have to get this dressed up for tonight."

"I'm taking my fiancée to her first Broadway musical." He slides his hands into mine. "It needs to be done right."

It will be done right.

I know what he has planned for me.

Gunner let it slip when I met him for lunch yesterday. I promised I wouldn't say anything to his boss.

Tonight, I'll sit next to my fiancé while I watch my first musical. Once the theater has cleared, we are going to go backstage to meet the cast. They'll soften the lights, clear a path and while the orchestra plays, I'll dance on a Broadway stage for the first time in the arms of the man I love.

"I love you, Dylan." I brush my lips over his. "Thank you for finding me again."

He deepens our kiss. "I love you."

I inch back and look into his eyes. "Promise that you'll keep me."

"I promise. You're mine." He glides a finger over my cheek. "That will never change."

That's not open for negotiation. I want to be Dylan's forever until the end of time.

ALSO BY DEBORAH BLADON
& SUGGESTED READING ORDER

HUSH

BARE

WISH

SIN

LACE

THIRST

COMPASS

VERSUS

RUTHLESS

BLOOM

RUSH

CATCH

FROSTBITE

XOXO

HE LOVES ME NOT

BITTERSWEET

THE BLUSH FACTOR

BULL

THANK YOU

Thank you for purchasing and downloading my book. I can't even begin to put to words what it means to me. If you enjoyed it, please remember to write a review for it. Let me know your thoughts! I want to keep my readers happy.

For more information on new series and standalones, please visit my website, deborahbladon.com

There are book trailers and other goodies to check out.

If you want to chat with me personally, please LIKE my page on Facebook. I love connecting with all of my readers because without you, none of this would be possible. www.facebook.com/authordeborahbladon

Thank you, for everything.

ABOUT THE AUTHOR

Deborah Bladon has never read a romance hero she didn't like. Her love for romance novels began when she was old enough to board the bus, library card in hand to check out the newest Harlequin paperbacks. She's a Canadian by heart, and by passport, but you can often spot her in New York City sipping a latte and looking for inspiration for her next story. Manhattan is definitely her second home.

She cherishes her family and believes that each day is a gift for writing, for reading, and for loving.

Made in the USA
Las Vegas, NV
14 January 2024

84374655R00152